Afterlife in the Attic

Spooky Shanty Realty Mysteries

B I Skinner

Acknowledgments

For Fufu and Albus and Pippi

Contents

1. Chapter 1 1
2. Chapter 2 6
3. Chapter 3 11
4. Chapter 4 17
5. Chapter 5 22
6. Chapter 6 28
7. Chapter 7 32
8. Chapter 8 36
9. Chapter 9 41
10. Chapter 10 45
11. Chapter 11 49
12. Chapter 12 55
13. Chapter 13 62
14. Chapter 14 67
15. Chapter 15 71
16. Chapter 16 76
17. Chapter 17 82
18. Chapter 18 90

19. Chapter 19 95
20. Chapter 20 101
21. Chapter 21 105
22. Chapter 22 111
23. Chapter 23 117
24. Chapter 24 124
25. Chapter 25 130
26. Chapter 26 135
27. Chapter 27 140
28. Chapter 28 145
29. Chapter 29 149
30. Chapter 30 155
31. Chapter 31 163
32. Chapter 32 167
33. Chapter 33 172
34. Chapter 34 176
35. Chapter 35 183
More Books by B I Skinner 185
Copyright 187

1

"Buster, go get Jake. We're late for school." Buster, our enormous black and white spotted Great Dane, frowns at me, sighing loudly. I didn't make that up. He legit frowned at me. I swear that dog understands me.

Why must she interrupt my naps?

Bit by bit he lumbers up the stairs, emphasizing just how annoyed he is that I disrupted his slumber. What does he have to complain about? He has all morning to sleep.

"Hey! Cut it out, Buster!" Jake complains. "All right, all right, I'm going. Just let me finish this last piece."

"You can finish after school!" I shout up the stairwell. That kid is so easily distracted. He gets it from his dad. He'd spend all day reading, building model cars, or playing video games if I didn't remind him to eat, sleep, and get dressed.

"Okay, I'm going," he grumbles while Buster shoulders all 150 canine pounds into him, to push him out of his room. He has a shoe on one foot, the other is in Buster's mouth.

"Moooooom, Buster is picking on me!" he whines while Buster pushes him toward the stairs.

"Thank you," I tell them when they finally reach the bottom while Buster drops the shoe at Jake's feet.

I swear I have to do everything around here.

He unleashes another loud sigh before flopping onto his fluffy bed in the sunny window.

“Do you have your homework?“

“Oops, I forgot it,“ he declares, heading back up the stairs.

“Nothing doing, mister.“ I grab the back of his T-shirt before he can go anywhere. He’ll just get distracted by his model car if I let him return to his room.

“Fine!“ Wearing a pinched expression he utters a retrieval incantation, making his homework float gently from his room, down the stairs, and into his waiting hands. He’s a wizard like his dad. I avoid encouraging magic at his age, but we’re already late for school, so I’ll make an exception this morning.

It doesn’t help that he’s astonishingly gifted. Too gifted if you ask me. That’s why, after finalizing the divorce, we enrolled him in the Petermore Academy. He’s still disorganized and easily distracted, but the academy has been so much better for his schoolwork and magic skills.

I worried when he started causing trouble in his old school. I was sure it was the divorce. However, the school counselor insisted he was bored and perhaps a new school was in order? Thankfully, she was right. Petermore has been so good for him. Now if I can figure out a way to make mornings easier, we’re set.

“Do you have everything?“ I press.

“Yep!“ He hops up and down to put his other shoe on. His short, sandy blonde hair is disheveled, as usual. Should I tell him to comb it? Nah. It’s not like he cares. I’m trying to be the mom who doesn’t nag about every little thing. But it’s hard sometimes!

"See you later, Buster!" Jake calls out before closing the door behind us. Buster tells us he's over it all by responding with an extra loud snore.

I thought they'd never leave.

"So, what happens if you didn't pass your test?" he asks during the drive to school.

"Oh, I passed it." I smile, all-knowing.

"You know, because you're trying to think positively, or you *know*?" He wiggles his fingers in the air.

"I know because I know," I respond, wiggling my own fingers about.

"Mom! You cheated?"

"Of course not!" It would have been easy to cheat because I'm part clairvoyant, part psychic. But what fun is that? I wanted to pass the exam for my real estate license fair and square.

But as the proctor fed the pages into the grading scanner, I had a vision of the real estate school handing me my license. I didn't see the score though, so perhaps I only passed by one question. But it's definitely a pass.

They don't tell us the results right away, which is a serious bummer. They make us return to the school for those. Then they hand us our new license or schedule a retake.

"I'm proud of you, mom. It's about time you did something for yourself," Jake says. "You spend a lot of time taking care of us. This is a chance for you to focus on yourself for a change. And you look really nice today by the way. Like someone who has an important job."

"Well, thanks, Jake. That's awfully sweet of you." What did I tell you? He's almost too smart.

"Then, when you make a bunch of money selling real estate, you can buy me a dirtbike for my next birthday."

Of course, there's a catch. "You keep dreaming, son," I tell him, reaching over to ruffle his hair even though he ducks out of the way.

"Make good choices!" I call after him while he hurries up the walkway to his waiting friends. He barely let me stop the car before jumping out. How is he growing up so fast?

I swear it was just yesterday I held that swaddled bundle of joy so snug in my arms. I was his entire world. Now he runs from the car, embarrassed that his friends might see me trying to smooth down his untamable cowlick.

But now I'm off to Melioras Village Real Estate School to pick up my license; then to Spooky Shanty Realty for my first day as a real estate agent. My new boss, Leon Lange, promised me a listing already.

"Assuming you pass the test, of course," he chuckled at my job interview last week.

I didn't tell him I already knew I passed. Even in a paranormal village like this one, where magical people outnumber nonmagicals, some are nervous about my gifts.

They don't believe me when I tell them that I avoid reading people. It's stressful for me and rude to them. Of course, that isn't to say that I won't ever use it when negotiating a deal for a new client. I'm required to act in their best interests, after all.

The blare of a car horn, along with screeching brakes, jerks me from my daydream about being the best real estate agent ever. A gray car swerves, barely missing mine.

The dark, heavily tinted windows prevent me from seeing who's inside. But the dark and, dare I say it, evil energy that passes through me as the car drives by unnerves me so much I shiver.

That near accident wasn't my fault, was it? I double check the light. No, whoever that was, they were definitely in the wrong.

I breathe deep, trying to center myself after I slide into an open spot in the parking lot at the real estate school. It's hard to shake off the dark energy, but after several moments of focus, I feel better. You are calm, composed, and confident, I remind myself. I'm ready to start my new life.

2

Taking a final deep breath to steady my nerves, I jog up the cement walkway toward the squatty looking, red-brick, real estate school.

Now that I'm here, I can barely contain my excitement. Jake and I are doing so well in our new lives. It's exactly what we needed.

It's a struggle to contain my exuberance when I approach the front desk. I remind myself I'm a professional now, so I should act like one. Or at least, like I *think* a professional should act.

The young, lavender-haired receptionist drags her attention from the game she's playing on her phone. She stares at me unblinkingly through her sparkly pink glasses.

After chomping for several seconds on a sizeable piece of blue gum, she blows an immense bubble. I don't think she recognizes me, despite my taking classes here every night for six weeks.

"Hi! I'm here to pick up, erm, check to see if I passed my real estate exam."

"Name?" she sighs as if I was interrupting something important. She could be Buster in human form!

"Molly Fitzle."

Using her feet to slowly roll her chair to the computer monitor, the squeaky wheels sound unnaturally loud in the quiet waiting room. I feel like I'm watching the sloth from Zootopia at work.

"How is that spelled?" she mumbles while glancing repeatedly at the clock.

Holding back a grimace, I count to three in my head. There's no need to antagonize this girl. I just want to collect my license and get out of here. I'm so eager to start my new job I can barely stand it. If only she were excited too!

"F - i - t - z - l - e," I enunciate while she pokes at the keyboard with an agonizingly slow, one-finger-at-a-time typing style.

She blows another enormous bubble, sucking it in rapidly before turning to me. "Looks like you failed."

"Excuse me?" I shriek in disbelief.

"Happens all the time. You have to schedule a retake."

Before I can protest further, she painstakingly returns her chair to the front of the desk. The squeaky wheels work my last nerve. Haven't they heard of WD40 in this office?

"I'm sorry, but that's impossible. I didn't fail," I assure her.

"Yes, you did," she responds, gritting her teeth at me. If she thinks she's losing patience with me, she should see the inside of my head.

"I know I passed. Can you please double-check?"

"You failed. It's not that big of a deal. Are you available next Thursday to retake it?" She points a perfectly manicured nail to a list of dates on her desk.

I could tell her I'm a psychic; therefore, I *know* I passed, but I'm not sure it would make a difference to her. Even worse, like Jake, she could assume I cheated and report me.

If the licensing board even *suspects* I cheated, I don't know what could happen, but I'm sure it isn't good. Who knows, maybe they could ban me from ever holding a license.

Whenever I tell someone I'm psychic, they mistakenly assume I'm reading their mind. When I tell them I'm also clairvoyant, the non-magicals always ask for winning lottery numbers.

But neither of my gifts works like that. They aren't *that* precise. Yes, I'm highly perceptive. Yes, I can sense when most people are lying, but I rarely know exactly what they're lying about. Then there's times when I see images.

When I was a kid, I saw one of my friends get hit by a car in a vision. I was so scared I ran two blocks to his house where I found him and his friends trying to pry open a manhole cover in the middle of the street.

I yelled at them to get out of the street, but they just shook their heads at me. It was enough to alert them though because seconds later a drunk driver careened around the corner, heading straight for them. They ran for cover while the driver plowed into a 100-year-old sycamore tree.

What did I get for my efforts though? Grounded. My mom completely freaked out when she heard the crash and realized I was missing. My friend always claimed they would have seen the car coming anyway.

See what I mean? The gift of sight isn't all it's cracked up to be.

Not everyone believes me when I tell them I go out of my way *not* to read people. I haven't always been this disciplined. It was much harder to block out all the incoming messages when I was younger.

It was overwhelming receiving everyone's thoughts and feelings. A crowded event could send my anxiety through the roof. Believe me, you don't want to know what most people are thinking.

"Could I please see the manager?" I request using a carefully managed tone.

Casting an exaggerated sigh at me, while blowing another bubble which I desperately want to reach out and pop, she stands up, and glares at me like I'm the worst person she's ever encountered. "I'll be right back."

This is the start of a new life for me. I was a stay-at-home mom before the divorce. We still have plenty of money between alimony and child support. We should. Zach, my ex, makes oodles of it. That was part of the problem. All he ever did was work. Oh, and hook up with his 23-year-old secretary.

I tiptoe several steps down the hallway attempting to hear the receptionist.

"Hey dad..."

Oh great.

"...there's someone out front who wants to see you."

Try as I might, I can't make out dad's response. His voice isn't shrieky like his daughter.

"I told her she failed her test, but she insists I'm wrong."

There's another pause where I know they're arguing, but I still don't know what he's saying.

"I tried rescheduling her, but she insists on seeing a manager."

She emphasizes manager like it's a ridiculous request, and she can't believe she's even saying it.

Upon hearing the creak of a leather chair, I hurry back to the front of the desk before they can catch me. Dad follows his daughter down the hallway. He's wearing a well-fitting pin striped suit and too much hair gel for my tastes. He doesn't look happy to be pulled away from whatever it was he was doing before his daughter came to get him.

"How can I help you?" he asks flashing a well-practiced smile.

"I came to get my exam results." I smile back, hoping that will soothe him and get us all on the right track.

"I told you already. You failed," she snaps. Her dad places a calming hand on her shoulder while she jabs her finger at the monitor.

"You're Monty Fitzpatrick?" he asks.

"What? No! I'm Molly Fitzle. F - i - t - z - l - e." I struggle to keep from shouting out the letters. Although that would be better than crying, like I'm also afraid I'm about to do.

My ex hated it when I cried. "What's wrong *now*?" he'd ask impatiently. Which always made me feel worse. As if I was a weak person for crying.

Sometimes a person just needs to cry. Right now, I'm trying my best to remain patient, but this isn't going at all as I planned. I hope this isn't a sign of things to come.

I retake slow, calm breaths while dad types in my *correct* name. Upon seeing the test results, he glares at his daughter.

"My apologies for the confusion, Ms. Fitzle. Congratulations! You passed."

3

After accepting the school manager's sincere apology and his daughter's not-so-sincere one, I snatch my license from his outstretched hand and run to my car. I'm so excited to finally get to work!

I don't even care anymore that the daughter almost gave me a stroke, thinking that I had somehow psychically misread the test results. Besides, I didn't just pass; I passed easily. I got an 89 when I only needed a 70; thank you very much.

It's all water under the bridge now. The important part is that I have my license, and I'm officially a real estate agent! As badly as I want to floor the gas pedal now, I remind myself to drive carefully. I don't need another close call like I had earlier.

The Spooky Shanty Realty office is an aged, haunted mansion converted into real estate offices. The ghost I had a lovely conversation with when I was here last week for my job interview gives me the thumbs up from a third-story window. When I return his thumbs up, he claps his luminescent hands. I told him I knew I had passed the test, but I don't think he believed me.

I climb the thick, gray, stone steps, deliberately placing my feet one at a time, like I'm marching into my new office. I'm so proud. And so excited. And so nervous! I've spent the last ten years doting on my family. It's like I forgot I existed. Now it's my time to shine.

"Hello, Mr. Lange. I got my license," I announce, poking my head into Leon Lange's, my new boss's office. I wave it about like it's a major award. It kind of is to me.

"Huh?" he grunts.

Why is he staring at me like he's never met me? This can't be good.

"I'm Molly Fitzle, a new agent. You interviewed me last week."

"Oh, uh, yeah, see if you can find an empty cubicle for your things," he mumbles, dismissing me with a wave of his thick, round hand. During our interview last week, he told me he once had lots of wavy, black hair, but working in real estate turned it gray. I hope he was kidding.

"Thank you so much! I'm eager to get started. I really appreciate the opportunity."

"Mmmm."

I leave him squinting at his computer screen while I wander away in search of a cubicle. Imagine that. Me with my very own cubicle. I can't wait to personalize it.

A picture of Jake to start. One where he isn't making some goofy face like he usually does. A plant would also liven things up. Maybe a Peace Lilly.

We can't have one at home because Buster would try to eat it. As if that enormous dog doesn't already eat plenty. Oh, if I have time, I'll also stop at the store today for a frame for my license.

Carefully placing my purse and license in the first empty cubicle I come across, I sigh contentedly. Then I change my mind and prop the license up against the side of the desk. That will do for now.

When I step back to admire it, a man barks, "That's taken!" so sharply that I jump almost a foot in the air.

I spin around, staring up at him in embarrassment. “I’m sorry, it looked empty.“

“Well, it’s not!“

“How about this one?“ My face burns with shame as I snatch my license from the desktop. I should know better. A professional would ask someone first.

“That’s taken too,“ he grunts.

Thunderation! This guy is playing with me.

“Would you please point me to an available cubicle?“ I ask in an amiable tone, hoping to smooth things over when what I really want to do is give him a good pinch. None of this is going as I pictured my first day should.

“Nope!“ He sneers, giving me the once over. He isn’t checking me out. It’s his version of a power play. He wants me to think my casual but pretty sundress is inappropriate. Yes, I’m using my gift to read him. Sometimes it’s necessary!

That reading tells me his outward appearance is all done deliberately to impress. The perfectly coifed hair and professional manicure. The three-piece designer suit, along with the half-windsor knot in his tie, and carefully placed matching pocket square are all for show. When he isn’t working, he prefers wearing baggy sweatpants and a stained t-shirt while he watches Buffy re-runs and eats tater tots. But no one else knows that. Not even his girlfriend.

I promise myself that if - make that *when* - I make it big, I’ll never look at someone like that. Especially a new agent who’s clearly nervous! I hate that he intimidates me. Just because he’s experienced and wealthy shouldn’t make me someone he looks at like a piece of gum he accidentally stepped in.

I smooth my sundress down in embarrassment. What I thought was so pretty and cheerful this morning seems frumpish now.

He thinks I'm just a divorced, rapidly approaching middle-aged housewife who got her license because she had no other worthwhile training. I worked in a bookstore for several years before Jake was born, but after that, I couldn't bear to tear myself away from that sweet little boy, so I happily stayed home with him.

Sure, I volunteered for Parent Teacher Council at school and always brought orange slices to his soccer games, but even I was restless at times. Helping at Jake's school was important, and the teachers were grateful, but it wasn't the same as working at a job that I'd gotten on my own.

When Jake surprised me by encouraging me to do something for myself, I jumped at the chance.

My embarrassment grows when Mr. Grumpy Pants leaves me standing there, embarrassed and unwanted, my new license clutched in my hands. He wanders back down the hallway without so much as a "see you later" to me.

"Another new one!" he grumbles to someone in an office, jerking his thumb in my direction.

"Oh, great!" comes the sarcastic reply.

This is definitely not how I saw this going when I left the house this morning.

But when I turn around, I'm grateful to see a woman in a cubicle talking on the phone. She's a pixie and she's beautiful. Her hair is blush colored and her skin is luminescent pink. Her wings are shaped like a butterfly with a rainbow of colors and glitter. Long, dark eyelashes frame her ruby eyes. I can't stop staring at them. I desperately want to touch them, they're so breathtaking but that would be rude.

She smiles encouragingly at me. I want to say something to her, but her phone call looks serious. When she smiles again and points to the empty cubicle beside hers, I happily put my things down.

“Thank you!” I mouth to her.

She nods, her attention still on the call. I sit down at my new cubicle, hoping she’ll finish soon so we can talk.

“Molly!“ Mr. Lange shouts from his office.

Finally! Time to work.

I hurry to his office, relieved that I finally have a cubicle and hopefully a new friend. “Hello, Mr. Lange!“

“Settling in, okay?“

“Yes. Well, kind of.“

“Let me guess. That old sourpuss Myers told you none of the cubicles were available. Just ignore him. Are you ready for your first listing?“

“Yes, sir!“

“It’s the old Baker house on Rosemary Street.“

“Didn’t Mr. Baker pass away recently?“

“He sure did. His only heir is a niece, Maureen, who lives out of state. She hired a company to clean out the house and get it ready to sell.“

“So, it’s vacant?“

“Yep. You’ll need to order yard signs right away.”

Once again, my cheeks color with embarrassment. I already ordered my signs. I knew I passed the test and would start work when I picked up my license, so why not?

“That’s already taken care of,” I stammer.

He raises a bushy eyebrow at my presumptuous move, but thankfully doesn’t question it. I want to fit in around here, not tip everyone off to my magical abilities right away.

I know from experience that people will avoid me at first when they find out what I can do. Witches, wizards, pixies, werewolves, and ghosts are plentiful in Melioras but my combination as a clairvoyant and psychic is unusual.

“That’s perfect because you already have a showing this afternoon. A family of vampires is moving here from Pittsburgh. Be at the property at 2:00.”

“Yes, sir!“ I exclaim.

"I’ll order the fliers for you now. You can pick them up at Stanley’s Sign Shop when you get your signs."

“I’ll go there right away.”

“Go get em girl!” the ghost shouts to me on my way out the door. I give him another jubilant thumbs up.

This is so exciting.

4

I hum along with the radio as I drive to the sign shop. What a gorgeous spring day! The sun is shining, the birds are singing, and the sky is a sparkling azure blue. Azure? I've never even used that word! Who cares how my day started? It's looking up in a big way!

The first time I drove through Melioras Village, I knew I wanted to live here. Picture a quaint London village you see in the movies. Winding roads, large chunky pots bursting with colorful spring flowers on every corner, round buildings made from thick bricks that don't match, it's all just perfect. I love it so much.

Jake's dad, Zach, lives about 20 minutes away in the next village – Aletara Porta. It's a nice place too, but not as nice as Melioras. I wanted Jake to be near his dad's place. Even though I'd rather be at least three states away, Jake needs his dad.

I'm still humming when I park my SUV in front of the sign shop, but my perfect moment screeches to a halt when I see them across the street. You'd hear a record needle scratching across the album if this were a movie.

It's my ex-husband, Zach, and his girlfriend. Who are also enjoying this perfect spring day at the Calimaris Coffee Shop.

I pretend I don't see them when my husband - I mean ex-husband - shouts. "Molly! Molly!"

I slowly turn around with what I hope is a convincing look of surprise. I wave back but continue toward the sign shop. I have important business to attend to, after all.

"Molly!" he calls out again, waving me over.

Balderdash! For Jake's sake, I suppose I should be cordial. What is his girlfriend's name. Tiffani? Bambi? Phoebe? The least he could do is date someone old enough to run for Congress.

She shifts in her chair uncomfortably. She should. He swears nothing happened before we split, but I suspect he's lying. He's a talented wizard, though, always blocking my attempts to read him, so who knows what really happened?

"What's up?" I ask as cheerfully as I can muster while Destini and I exchange polite hellos.

"Jake told me you got your real estate license."

"That's right." I puff up with pride. "I'm on my way to get the yard signs for my first listing right now."

"I take it Jake got to school okay this morning?" he asks as if my having a job now means Jake has dropped out of school and is left to wander the streets.

"He got to school just fine," I respond testily.

"What if he gets sick and you have to show a house?"

"Then I'll call Mrs. Moore to babysit like we always have." Mrs. Moore is an angel. A literal angel who's been like a surrogate grandparent to Jake ever since he was born. Her own grandchildren live several hours away by plane, so she doesn't get to see them as often as she likes. She gets grandbaby time with Jake, and I get a much-needed break when I need it.

"The new school seems to agree with him," Zach points out.

"Yes," I smile, broadly. "He's doing so much better. Although he's still a disorganized, easily distracted pre-teen."

Zach grimaces. "He gets that from me."

"Don't I know it." Ariel crosses her arms and pinches her lips when we share an easygoing laugh. Our marriage wasn't all bad. We had lots of good times. We just married too young. Had we met five years later, who knows?

"It was lovely to see you both," I tell them as sincerely as I can, "but I have to go now. I have a house to sell."

I cross the street again to Stanley's Sign Shop, refusing to let them get me down. I may have encountered more obstacles than I thought I would on my first day, but I'm going to sell the heck out of this house!

When I step into the shop, and a wizard who I assume is Stanley greets me, we're interrupted by my buzzing pocket. What now?

Lunch? my sister Anne texts.

Sure, what time?

Noon?

I'll be there! I passed my exam, of course.

I knew you would! Although you knew you would, too! LOL! You didn't cheat, did you?

Of course not! I'm picking up my yard signs for my first listing now.

That's great! I'm so proud of you.

Thanks! See you at noon.

I almost include a snotty comment about Zach and Trixi but decide against it. He just isn't worth it. But maybe Anne remembers her real name.

"Sorry about that." I apologize to Stanley. "It was my sister."

"No problem. I have three of those myself. So, what do you think?" he asks. When he raises his hand, three large aluminum signs float from the back room.

They feature a cottage, with a sold sign out front, then the trademark colors of Spooky Shanty Realty - purple and mango. Underneath the tagline it reads, “Molly Fitzle, Sales Associate.” I grin, swelling with pride. Look at me, a full-fledged businesswoman.

“They’re perfect!“ I tell him.

“Here’s the flyers that Mr. Lange ordered as well. You’re selling the Baker house, huh?“ he asks, handing me a flat box full of colorful flyers.

“It’s my first listing!“ I smile so big my face hurts.

“Congratulations and good luck.“

“Thank you!”

“If you’ll get the door, I’ll move the signs straight into your SUV.”

I hold open the shop door, pressing the button on my key fob to open the back door of my Volkswagen Taos. It’s the perfect size for me. Just right for hauling Jake and all of his things and now my real estate supplies.

Bobbi watches the process from across the street as the signs gently stack themselves in my vehicle. I resist the urge to stick my tongue out at her. I know. Sometimes I can be so childish.

After glancing at my watch, I realize I have just enough time to run over to the Baker house, put my sign and flyers in the yard, then do a quick walkthrough, so I’ll know where everything is before I actually show it.

It’s a cozy looking house with two floors, a small patio, and cheerful snapdragons lining the walkway. It could use some flowerpots on the porch though.

After popping the back door open and grasping one of the for sale signs, I realize they’re heavier than I thought. It’s times like this that I wish I were a witch. A little magic could go a long way here.

I feel ridiculous struggling to plant the sign in the yard. Not so easy with heels on, I can tell you. I thought this would be a lot easier. I imagined myself planting the sign into the yard with one big satisfying flourish. It seems like a lot of things aren't going like I anticipated.

Taking a quick glance around me to make sure no one is watching, I jump up and down on the bar across the bottom of the sign to push it into the ground. I work up a sweat struggling with it, but when it's finally in place, I pop the flyers into the flyer box, stepping back to admire my handiwork. It's gorgeous! I snap a quick picture for my Facebook page, then head to the front door.

Thankfully, Mr. Lange remembered to text me the code to the lockbox on the front door when I was in the sign shop.

But just as I enter the first number, my phone rings.

"Hey, Jake! What's up?"

"Mom! I'm in trouble!"

5

"Mom! I forgot my soccer uniform. We have a game this afternoon!"

Ugh.

"I asked you last night if you had a game today, but you said no."

"I didn't think I did!"

"Can't you go without the uniform? Play in your gym clothes."

"I can't play in the game if I don't have my uniform."

I swear, this kid. "All right. I'll run home to get it."

"And my cleats."

"Okay."

"And my shin guards."

"Of course. Jake, I hope you realize you can't be doing this now that I'm working."

"This is the last time, I swear!"

"No doubt." I guess I won't see the inside of the house until the showing appointment. I really wanted to look like I know what I'm doing in front of the buyers, but I don't want Jake to think I'm neglecting him just because I'm working. No need to give Zach another excuse to complain. I'll just have to fake it with the vampires.

“Forget something?“ Oliver, our 300 year old house poltergeist asks when I rush through the front door, out of breath from hurrying. We just bought the house a month ago. I didn’t realize there was a poltergeist living here until we moved in.

The real estate agent suggested we get a Spirit Inspection, but I declined. I didn’t sense any other-worldly beings the first time he showed it to us, so I didn’t think it was necessary. Little did I know the poltergeist was out wandering along the road, terrorizing unsuspecting motorists while we were looking at the house.

“Jake forgot his soccer uniform.“

“Oh, I could’ve told you that.“

“Then why didn’t you?“ I snap.

“I didn’t feel like it,“ he says before disappearing with a pop. It’s bad enough that I live with a 10-year-old who’s going on 30. I also have a cantankerous poltergeist to contend with. I’ve considered hiring a medium to get rid of him, but I haven’t had the time.

“Watch it, or I’ll get some sage,” I call out.

“That doesn’t work on me,“ he shouts back from the ether with a cackle.

I search for Jake’s uniform in the disaster he calls a bedroom. The kid can literally do magic, but his bedroom still looks like a tornado blew through here. I finally locate his jersey under the bed. I don’t want to think about the last time he washed it. Scratch that; *I* washed it.

Where would I be if I were a soccer cleat? Closet? Oh, look, there’s one. Now, where’s the other? Ah ha! Under the desk. Now for the shin guards. We have got to get organized if I’m working full-time.

I won't have all day to follow this kid and clean up after him. There's the shin guards and shorts on the fishtank. At least he's good about caring for the fish. I stuff it all in a gym bag and dash out the door again, leaving Buster still snoring in the sunny window.

I don't think he knew I was even there. Heaven help us if we're ever robbed. Buster would show them where everything is, if it meant they would leave him alone so he could get back to his nap.

I drive to Jake's school again, continuously glancing at my watch. When I pull up in front, I practically fling Jake's things out the window. I'll barely be in time for lunch with Anne.

I'm still so mad at myself I didn't have the chance to go through the house before showing it. Jake and I will talk this weekend about how things are different now. He's ten. There are some things he'll have to learn to do for himself. I may need to give him more leeway with magic and the chores.

I finally get to Barties Bistro anxious and out of breath. "Hi! I'm meeting Anne Simon."

"I don't see anyone with that name on here," the host says, consulting the list on the stand.

Great, I raced over here for nothing.

"Would you like to be seated while you wait?" she asks.

"Yes, please!"

I'm grateful for the chance to catch my breath while gathering my thoughts. I make a note on my phone to buy some pretty flowers for the patio of the Baker house. I want it to look cheerful and inviting.

What if the vampires fall in love with it immediately, and I don't have to worry about flowers? Wouldn't Mr. Grumpy Pants and his designer suit be surprised?

Just think of it. A sale from my first showing! That would be an incredible start. Don't get your hopes up, I tell myself. A sale that fast would be unusual, I'm sure.

"What can I get you to drink?" a fairy no bigger than a coffee cup asks me.

"Iced tea would be great."

"Coming right up."

Even though I pretend to scan the menu, I already know what I'm getting. I always tell myself I'll try something different here, but then I don't. I must have been daydreaming about my first home sale longer than I realized because it's already 12:30. Where is that darn sister of mine? I'll have to remind her as well that I have a job now and can't sit around and wait for everyone.

The other diners come and go, but no Anne. If I skip lunch and leave now, I would have just enough time to pick up some flowers and go through the house before the appointment. She's the one who invited me to lunch, anyway.

I've never actually done that. Leave when someone else is late. Would it be too rude? I'll give her ten more minutes, but then that's it, I swear. It would serve her right for always being late.

After another 15 minutes with no Anne and no explanatory text, I tell the waiter I won't stay for lunch after all, and could he tell me what I owe for the iced tea? When I get up to leave, I drop a generous tip on the table for wasting his time when, of course, my sister rushes in. Now *she's* the one who's out of breath. Her flushed, sweaty face has a smudge of dirt on it.

We have the same long, red hair, but hers reminds me of Jake's hair this morning, all unruly and wild. When was the last time she combed *her* hair? And is that a stick poking out from the back? What the heck happened to her?

"Where have you been?" I scold her.

"Don't ask!" she says. "Sorry I'm late!"

"Are you okay?"

"I'm fine!" she insists.

"No, you aren't." I can sense her distress. She's lying.

"You better not be reading me!" she scolds.

"A person doesn't have to be psychic to see something is wrong," I point out grumpily.

"Okay, if you must know, I lost track of time as usual, but I didn't want you to lecture me, so I ran down the street and tripped and fell. I even broke my shoe." She waves her broken shoe in front of me.

I know it's rude to read my sister, but it's not like I want to know what she got me for Christmas. If I thought she was in danger, wouldn't I be obligated to use my gifts to help?

Of course, she's blocking me because she's a witch. A healing witch to be exact. She isn't as powerful as Zach or even Jake. Her powers involve healing spells using magic. She also owns the most popular crystal and potion shop in the village.

"Hang on a second, were you leaving?" she asks when she sees the tip on the table. "Don't tell me you had lunch without me!"

"I should have! You're an hour late!"

"I told you I was sorry. C'mon. Just sit down and order. You can tell me all about how your first day of real estate is going."

"It's been a bit hectic!" I groan, slumping back in my chair. I really should be firm and tell her I don't have time, but instead I order a monte cristo sandwich, fries, and coleslaw, hoping it will be quick to prepare.

I'm so nervous about the showing that I wasn't sure I could eat, but when the waiter levitates my lunch to the table, forcing a passerby to duck first, and the smell of hot, fried, salted potatoes tickles my nose,

I realize I'm famished. It's probably best that I eat something now, so my stomach isn't growling when I show the house.

Anne looks at me funny when I inhale my lunch, but luckily for her, she doesn't comment on it. I explain everything that's happened so far today. She doesn't remember Zach's girlfriend's name either. She suggests Rubi but I don't think that's it.

As soon as I finish eating, I apologize for being in a rush, but I refuse to be late for the showing. I leave the bill with her and race out the door. Her mouth drops open in surprise at my bold move. Serves her right. I'm ready for my first showing!

6

I congratulate myself when I realize I'll actually be about ten minutes early to the showing appointment. I'll still have a few minutes to go through the house before the buyers arrive.

Congratulations quickly turns to anxiety, however, when I pull up in front of the house only to realize the vampires are already there. Oh, no! What if they think I'm late? What a horrible impression I'm already making.

Before you get hung up on the legend of vampires perishing in sunlight, or killing me for my blood, don't believe everything you've heard. They don't burst into flames the moment they're exposed to sunlight, although they do avoid direct exposure to it. This family is all wearing hats while waiting for me in the shade of the awning on the patio.

As for their blood source, I kind of don't want to think about it. I've heard they've made surprising advances in synthetic blood that the undead simply order online. I picture it being like veggie burgers for vegetarians.

Rest assured, they won't be chomping on me or anyone else this afternoon. I feel perfectly safe with them. Now if they just buy the house, it will make up for all this morning's disappointments.

"Good afternoon, Mr. and Mrs. Cabello! I hope you haven't been waiting long."

"Not to worry; we came early to look around. We were just checking out the yard and the neighborhood."

"Good idea! If you're ready to head inside, we can see what that's like as well."

They wait patiently for me to unlock the lockbox and then the front door. I want to ask them how old they really are but that would be rude. Mom and dad must have been bitten sometime in their 40's. Their son must be a teenager. It would be fascinating to know how long ago it was. But it's none of my business.

"Do you know if there are any ghosts in this house, dear?" Mrs. Cabello asks.

"I'm sorry, but I don't." Dang, it. If I had seen the house myself earlier, I'd know the answer to that.

"We've heard that having ghosts in the home can be a hassle," Mr. Cabello tells me.

I nod. "There's a poltergeist in my new house. He can be such a pill. But there are specialists you can hire to cleanse the house if it's a problem," I offer.

"That's good to know." Mrs. Cabello relaxes.

I smile at the sullen teenager standing with them. "No school today?" I ask, immediately regretting it.

"I'm 400 years old," he snaps.

"Yes, of course. How silly of me."

"Don't be rude!" his father chastises him.

What a delight that would be. A perpetual teen. Forever trapped at 16.

"I'll let you look around at your own pace. If you have questions, let me know," I explain, opening the door for them. "So far, I'm not sensing any ghosts. You should always have a thorough inspection, of course, to identify potential problems."

"That's excellent advice; oh, my goodness, look at this kitchen!" the wife exclaims, her concerns about ghosts all but forgotten.

I don't want to crowd them or make them think I'm impatient, so I do my best to fade into the background. They should form their own opinions. Besides, while they're busy in the kitchen, this is my chance to look elsewhere.

I might as well start with the attic. I'm sure it's the most boring part, anyway. A shockingly powerful wave of dark energy hits me the moment I put a foot on the first stair. It's so dark my knees buckle, forcing me to grab onto the stair railing. There's something in the attic and it's bad.

"Excuse me, Molly?" Mrs. Cabello calls out.

"Yes?" I hurry into the kitchen, eager to help, momentarily forgetting what I just sensed, even though my heart has sped up to an uncomfortable level. I'll answer her question, then get back to the attic to see what's going on there. I'm not receiving any images, just enough dark energy that it needs a closer look.

"Do you know what kind of wood they made these cabinets with?" she asks.

"It looks like walnut to me, but I can double-check on that if you want."

"They're gorgeous!" she says.

Relieved that it seems to be a good enough answer for now, I pull out my phone to make a note to ask Mr. Lange if he knows what the kitchen cabinets are made of while Mrs. Cabello heads for the attic.

"Wait! Just a moment!" I exclaim when I realize where she is.

Too late. Her terrified scream cuts through the house.

Mr. Cabello, their son Derrick, and I race for the attic stairs, where we grapple to get through the doorway all at once.

Mr. Cabello finally shoves past us, taking the attic stairs two at a time while Derrick and I are right behind him.

Mrs. Cabello's screaming reaches a fevered pitch. What could it be that's made her so upset? Did a wild animal sneak in? Is there a skunk in the attic? Hideous wallpaper? A hole in the roof? Given what I felt earlier, I know it can't be as easy as that, but one can always hope. Why is she still screaming?

Even though this is only my first showing, I'm pretty sure this isn't supposed to happen. When Mr. Cabello curses, I know for certain this shouldn't happen.

For a moment I hope it isn't as bad as I imagine when Derrick shouts, "Wicked!"

But my hopes are smashed to smithereens as I choke back my own scream at the body lying in the middle of the attic, staring up at the ceiling with blank eyes, blood pooling under his head. Vomit threatens to sneak past the back of my throat when I realize it's Barney Mullins, my sister‘s ex-fiancé. So, it's a skunk, all right, but not the kind I was expecting.

"We're definitely not buying this house!“ Derrick exclaims with disgust.

7

Mrs. Cabello's screams continue bouncing off the attic walls. When she presses her hands against her eyes to keep from looking at the body, I berate myself for not knowing what to do in a situation like this. Questions build in my head like a dark, booming thunderstorm. Was the body here when I came earlier? I'm no coroner, but it doesn't look like he's been dead very long.

While Mrs. Cabello's shrieking intensifies, the rest of us stare at Barney, unable to move, unable to fully process what we're looking at.

"We didn't do this!" Derrick insists fiercely.

"I didn't think you did," I assure him.

My sister's late lunch arrival and her unkempt appearance flash through my head, but I quickly tamp it down. I have to be the one to tell her this. She can't hear it from someone else or worse, on the news. But I can't just tell her over the phone, can I? I'm worried the news will travel fast through this small town, though.

Mr. Cabello tries to calm down Mrs. Cabello, but it's no use. Derrick appears torn between wanting to punch something and getting a closer look at the body.

"Can't you do something about this?" He advances on me so quickly that I step back. When a tiny bit of fangs slip out, I throw my hand over my mouth to keep from gasping out loud. They did not cover this in real estate school!

"Derrick!" Mr. Cabello's voice cuts through the chaos. "Take your mother downstairs!"

He scowls, reluctantly following his father's orders.

"We need to call the authorities," Mr. Cabello insists.

"Yes, of course." I pull my cell phone from my pocket, willing my trembling hands to press the right buttons. What am I supposed to say at this point? Hi, I'm a horrible real estate agent, and I just discovered a body at my first listing. I can't bring myself to admit that it's my sister's ex-fiancé - not out loud anyway.

Instead, I explain to the operator that we're at 17 Rosemary Street and there's a body in the attic. I promise to stay on the scene, but not touch anything. My hands are still shaking so badly I can barely push the correct button to hang up. It's a wonder I didn't drop the phone; I'm so unnerved.

Still staring at Barney's body, the urge to touch him is overwhelming. Not because I'm morbid, but to see if I can get a psychic reading from it. I can't do it in front of Mr. Cabello, though. He'll think I'm out of my mind. Or worse - he might think I'm trying to cover up evidence.

He must have heard me tell the operator I won't touch anything. Yet, touching the body might tell me who did this or how it happened. It could at least give me a clue. Dare I risk it in front of Mr. Cabello? I take a small, slow step toward the body. If I could just...

"Let's go," he says when sirens pierce the air.

I should tell him I'm a psychic and if I touch the body I could see if there's any psychic energy left for me to read. But I don't. I just dutifully follow him out of the attic.

I shudder to think what Sheriff Blake will do when he realizes I'm the one who found his cousin's body. Yep, I said cousin.

After my sister caught Barney cheating on her, she called off the wedding. To say she had some issues after that is an understatement. She got a little crazy, as one might expect.

She slashed the tires on his car. Well, not really slashed. It's harder to cut through a tire than she realized. Especially when all she had was a dull steak knife from the kitchen drawer. As a healing witch she doesn't have the power to cast a spell to cut someone's tires. So, when the dull knife didn't work, she just let all the air out.

But that took so long, he caught her ducking behind the car. Then they had a screaming match in the middle of the street in front of numerous neighbors who finally called the Sheriff. But not before my sister threatened to kill Barney. Loudly.

Somehow, I managed to forget all of that until now. Why didn't I press her on the real reason she was late for lunch? I know she wasn't just late as usual like she claimed. She wouldn't care if she forgot the time and showed up late.

Normally, she wouldn't even apologize. The fact she offered an excuse today, in addition to being a complete mess, is a bad sign. I know my sister didn't kill Barney, but I also worry this could look really bad to everyone else.

Mr. Cabello and I step onto the porch just as Sheriff Blake arrives, his lips pinching with disdain the moment he sees me. When he pauses to discuss something with a deputy, they keep pointing at us and then at the attic. It's official. Worst first showing ever.

When the Sheriff advances on us, I gulp. He's a werewolf. A particularly large werewolf. I try to remember which moon cycle we're currently in. I think we just passed this month's full moon. I may not be afraid of vampires, but werewolves make me nervous.

Barney once told my sister that his cousin locks himself in a secure vault during the full moon, but what happens if he forgets? Or what if he doesn't get to the vault in time and loses control? I shudder when I think of werewolves running loose in the village. My imagination goes wild for a moment when I wonder if he accidentally killed Barney.

"What happened?" he asks. Even though Mr. Cabello and I are standing on the porch, and Sheriff Blake is three steps down, he's still taller than us.

"I was showing the house when we found a body." My voice is all squeaky and nervous. How do I tell him it's Barney?

"Did you touch anything?"

I shake my head. I still wish I could touch the body. If the energy is right, it could tell me who killed him.

"Who's here with you?"

"Just me and the Cabellos," I explain, pointing to Mr. Cabello next to me, then his wife and son in the middle of the yard, where Derrick is still trying to calm his hysterical mother.

"Don't even think about leaving," he tells us, signaling to another deputy who has arrived to assist with the investigation.

"Wait," I plead as he heads to the door. He glares at me so fiercely when I briefly touch his arm that I snatch my hand back like I accidentally touched a hot stove. He probably thinks I was trying to read him, but I swear I wasn't. I was just trying to get him to pause for a moment.

"The body..." I choke up.

"What?" he demands impatiently.

"It's Barney."

8

His face darkens while he throws the door open so hard it slams against the wall. Yikes!

Seconds later, another deputy arrives to take our statements. He purposely places us in different parts of the yard. When I ask him why, he explains they don't want witnesses influencing each other. It's not like we have much to tell, however. There's a body in the attic. End of story.

The sheriff's department knows my sister, which means they're no fans of mine. I may be new to Melioras, but they know who I'm related to.

"This is your listing, correct?" the deputy asks dispassionately.

"Yes."

"This is the first you noticed a body in the attic?"

I want to answer him with a sarcastic nah, it's been here for weeks, and I just now decided to call it in. Thankfully, I think better of it. "Yes. I just got my license today, along with this listing."

The deputy drones on endlessly with questions I don't really know how to answer. Yes, I stopped here earlier to place the for sale sign in the yard. No, I didn't enter the house at the time. No, I've never been inside until just now. I'm sure they think I'm stalling, but I can't help it. I don't have the answers they're looking for.

My primary concern right now is to get to my sister before anyone else does. Finally, the deputy tells me I'm free to leave the property but that I'm not allowed to leave town. Is he telling me I'm a suspect? Whatever. Obviously, I didn't do this.

Don't turn on the tv. I need to talk to you. I text Anne.

What's going on?

Just call me!

You'll have to wait. The store is full of people.

Bejeebers, why is she so stubborn? I hope one of her customers doesn't spill the beans before I can get over there. She owns the Curing Crystals & Potions Shop, a wildly popular store at the end of the village.

Just as I'm about to step off the patio, Sheriff Blake stomps out the front door, angrier than ever.

"Have you talked to your sister today?"

"Why?"

"Just answer the question."

"We had lunch."

"What time?"

I start to tell him that it was a later lunch than I expected because Anne held everything up, but instinct warns me to keep my mouth shut. I have a very bad feeling about this. "It was at 1:00."

He scribbles that down.

"Where?"

"Barties Bistro."

Again, he writes it down. I really need to leave, but I don't want him to think I'm running off to warn my sister.

My heart sinks when a deputy winds yellow crime scene tape around the house while the others comb the yard for clues.

When the local news station shows up with a camera, I groan in regret. Why did I put up my sign? Mr. Lange won't be happy to see this. Is this the shortest real estate agent tenure on record? I've only had my license for a few hours when my listing is seized by the authorities.

I'm so busy watching the news station photographer take pictures of my for sale sign that I'm startled when my phone buzzes with a text.

The store is swamped. Why don't you just come by?

I guess I'll have to. At least she's busy. Too busy to watch the news, I hope.

SCENE BR

When I hurry into Anne's crystal store, praying I'm not too late, I'm relieved to see she's happily interacting with a customer.

Anne's shop is always crowded for good reason. Looking for a rare ingredient for a potion to heal that nagging toothache? She'll have it. Craving a rose quartz to keep peace in your home while your in-laws visit? She'll have it. I don't know how she does it, but she snags those specialty ingredients no one else can.

Usually, I love visiting her shop. Row upon row of glowing jewel-colored potions stored in uniquely shaped bottles and jars, tables full of artfully arranged baskets with sparkling crystals, and thick, scented dazzling candles designed to assist even the most inexperienced witches and wizards with their spell needs.

There's always something to look at and admire in here. Today, however, I come with such awful news I don't notice the things in the shop. I just see the throngs of shoppers who need to pause for a moment so I can give Anne the news.

"I really need to talk to you," I whisper, taking her by the arm when the customer goes back to browsing. This isn't the ideal place to give her this kind of news, but it will have to do. She resists when I try to steer her into the back room.

"So, talk. Hey, how did your showing go?"

"That's what I need to talk to you about."

"Oh, my gosh, you sold it already! Your first showing! That's so exciting!"

"No, that's not exactly it."

"That's okay; better luck next time, right?"

"I'm serious! We need to talk." Why won't she just do what I say?

Before I can get her away from the customers, Sheriff Blake and two deputies march into the shop. Store activity comes to a standstill while an uneasy hush blankets the room.

"What is this about?" Anne asks, finally realizing I was serious when I was trying to get her attention. "Molly, what's going on?"

"Anne Simon you are under arrest for the murder of Barney Mullins."

"Hang on a second! Murder? Barney is dead?"

While the deputy cuffs her and reads her rights, everyone stares.

Right on cue, the news crew that was at the house blusters through the door.

Wonderful. Not only was a body found in my listing, my sister is being arrested for it.

My new boss is really going to be thrilled now. Just when I think this can't get any worse, I get a text from my new boss.

My office now!

Oh well, this was fun while it lasted, right? So long real estate career. I wonder if I can learn to type.

"Heck of a first day, huh, Molly?" Mr. Lange says when I reluctantly enter his office.

"I'm so sorry! I didn't know there was a body in the attic!"

"Obviously, you wouldn't have shown it if you knew."

Phew. This doesn't sound as bad as I thought.

"However..."

Uh Oh.

"I got a call from the real estate board. They've suspended your license, pending a hearing."

"They've what? I haven't even had it for a day!"

"I understand that, but as you know, part of holding a license in this state is you agree to exhibit good moral character. Apparently, discovering your sister's ex-fiancé's body during a showing is considered questionable. I'm sorry, but you can't practice real estate until after the hearing."

I trudge back to my cubicle, devastated. My license sits alone still propped against the plain wall. My plans for a plant, the picture of Jake, and the frame for my license seem so long ago. The problems at the real estate school this morning seem so petty now.

I had my license less than 24 hours. My sister is in jail for allegedly murdering Barney, but why? What kind of evidence could they have? Other than her hating Barney for cheating on her? This has to be a personal vendetta. Obviously, I know my sister didn't kill anybody.

Someone needs to investigate this thoroughly and not just assume my sister did it. Looks like that someone is me.

9

“Shame you were just getting started...“ Myers says radiating superiority when he sees me slumped in my cubicle, my head buried in my hands.

“Oh, buzz off!” the pixie I saw talking on the phone earlier tells him, shooing him away with a sweep of her hand.

“I can’t believe this happened to you! Are you okay? That must’ve been so scary on your first day!“

“So, this isn’t normal?“ I ask, partly in jest, because I’m sure it isn’t, yet I feel like I need to double check. I don’t know how I could handle any more dead bodies.

“I swear to you I have never found a body at a showing,“ she laughs.

“Good, because I was beginning to worry!“

“What did Mr. Lange say?“

“The real estate board has suspended my license pending a hearing.“

“Oh, no! You just got it too.“

“This isn’t at all like I pictured it when I decided to do this.”

“Murder is unusual, I promise,” she tells me with her hand up.

“Believe it or not, it isn’t just that. Although that would be plenty.”

“What do you mean?”

"In one short day, it's like everything that could go wrong did. There was a mixup at the real estate school with my license, then just as I think I'm ready to get started, that Myers guy treats me like dirt—"

"Don't mind him," she quickly interrupts. "He's always threatened by new and energetic agents."

"Why?" I ask. "He's obviously doing just fine. Why would someone like me be a threat?"

"He hates that things have changed so much. He misses the days when agents took the husband out for whiskey and cigars while showing him a stack of listings that only *he* knew about. Now buyers find homes online and contact *us*. Personally, I like it better this way."

"I can't say I'm big on whiskey and cigars."

"Me either," she laughs. "I'm Tina Lucas by the way."

"Molly Fitzle," I respond. But before she can say anything more, I blurt out, "This is all my fault."

"How is this your fault? Unless you murdered that guy."

"No, I didn't murder him! Although when we found out he was cheating on my sister, it crossed my mind." I clap my hand over my mouth. Did I really just say that? This is no time to be joking, but I couldn't help it.

Thankfully Tina just laughs. "I bet you did. But if you didn't kill him, how is any of this your fault?"

"Where do I start?" I ask in dismay.

"From the beginning. I have time."

Before I can stop myself, it spills out. "I got divorced, but I don't actually have to work, you know. I stayed home with my son for ten years, but I was looking for something important to do. It was actually my son who encouraged it. I still feel guilty about the divorce and even getting this new job.

"Then Jake, my son, who's freaky smart, but so forgetful, forgot his soccer uniform today, so I had to go home and get it, then take it to him at school. If I didn't have to do that, I could have looked at the house before the buyers did. I would have found the body, then called the sheriff's department and Mr. Lange.

"At least the Cabellos wouldn't have had to see the body. And the news reporters wouldn't have filmed Mrs. Cabellos having a panic attack. Then, of course, there's the footage of me at my sister's shop watching her get arrested. I swear if the real estate board reinstates my license, it will be a miracle. Although, maybe that's best. I should just stay home. At least as a stay at home mom, I never found any bodies."

"Whoa! Slow down there, sister."

"I'm so sorry! I shouldn't be talking like this. We just met."

"No, I don't mean that. I told you I had time to listen. What I meant was slow down on the self blame. For starters, you said your son is smart, right?"

"Too smart."

"I know when each of my kids were 10 years old there were some lessons they had to learn the hard way." When I look shocked, she quickly adds, "I don't mean life threatening hard way, I mean things like simple consequences."

"I don't understand."

"You said you asked him the night before if he had a game today, but he said no."

"Yes, exactly." I nod.

"So, he can't be trusted to keep track of which days are game days?"

"Well..."

"What if you had told him that because he didn't have his uniform, he had to sit this game out? Or call his dad. His dad was just in a coffee shop, hanging out with his girlfriend. Why couldn't dad have handled the uniform?"

"Well. I. Uh. I'm not sure what to say." I chuckle uneasily. She might be right. But I don't know if I'm ready to admit that.

"Of course, your sister didn't kill Barney. Sooner or later - my bet is sooner - the real killer will be discovered, you'll get your license back, and then you'll make an amazing real estate agent. I'll help."

"Thank you, I really appreciate your listening to me. Uh oh!" I exclaim when I realize what time it is. "I have to pick Jake up for his soccer game. Then I have to decide how to break the news to him about his aunt getting arrested."

"Well, go! It's important to be at the games, of course. But keep me posted, okay? Mr. Lange didn't say you can't come into the office, right?"

"No, he just said I can't practice real estate until the board reinstates my license."

"Then don't be a stranger. There's still plenty for you to learn until you get your license back."

I ignore the dirty looks Myers gives me as I leave the office. Despite all the horrible things that have happened today, and despite what I know will be an uphill battle, I feel a little better. I'm excited about making new friends. Friends who aren't just the wives of Zach's colleagues or moms from Jake's old school.

I have my own colleagues now! Sure, some might seem insufferable at the moment, but others are quickly becoming friends and mentors.

I don't know what to do next with Anne but it's important that I keep things as normal as possible with Jake for the time being. I have a bad feeling this will get a lot worse before it gets better.

10

When I get to Jake's school, I find him waiting alone on the front steps. Aargh! I am a horrible mother. When he sees me, he leaps up, running toward the car.

"Mom! Thank goodness you came!"

"I'm only a few minutes late; were you worried?"

"The kids said Aunt Anne killed somebody! It was on the internet and everything! You were there too! Why were you there? Is it because Anne did it? What happens next? Did you see the body? Was it all gross looking? They didn't show that part."

Questions fly fast and furious from his mouth I foolishly thought that I'd be able to tell him the story after dinner. What was I thinking? The kids all have smartphones these days that they can access at any time. Jake has a phone, but it's for emergencies.

"Did you really get to see a dead body?"

"Yes, unfortunately, I saw the body."

"Yikes!" he exclaims. "What did it look like? Did it look like a zombie?"

"No, it just looked like a dead body."

"Did Aunt Anne really kill him?"

"Of course not!"

"Is it true? It was Uncle Barney?"

“Yes, it was Barney.“

“The same guy Aunt Anne was engaged to.“

“Yup. That’s him.“

“I never liked that guy. But don’t tell anyone. My teacher said we shouldn’t speak bad about dead people. Or something like that,” he admits.

“Don’t tell anyone, but I didn’t like him either.“

“Did someone really kill him?“

I might as well tell him the truth. He’ll just hear about it somewhere else, anyway. “From what I could tell, yes, he had a nasty gash on his head.“

“But why do they think Aunt Anne did it?“

“That part I don’t know for sure.“

“Shouldn’t you find out?“ he asks.

“I’m working on it.”

“Cool. On TV, they ask for a lawyer. Does she have a lawyer?“

“Our cousin Harvey is a lawyer, but I haven’t had a chance to call him.”

“Is it because you’re too busy working now?“

I cringe when he says that. “I hope that your aunt has already called him.” I decide not to tell him I’ve been suspended. He doesn’t need to know everything this second. “Hopefully, the police will figure out quickly that it wasn’t your aunt.” It’s all I can come up with at the moment.

“There’s dad!“ Jake points out when we arrive at the soccer field. This day just gets better and better. It’s not that I want Zach to miss Jake’s games or anything, but I’d rather not have to *see* him, either. Thankfully, Trixi isn’t with him.

“Hey, dad!“ Jake runs straight for him, his hand outstretched. They high-five before he sprints the other direction to greet his teammates.

Is it just me, or are people staring at us? I take my time getting out of the car. I can already hear Zach’s complaints.

“What’s going on?” Zach snaps. “Is it true? Did your sister really murder Barney?“

“She didn’t murder him, obviously!“ I snap back, careful to make sure Jake can’t hear us arguing.

“Then why did they arrest her?“

“Have you never heard of innocent until proven guilty?“

“They obviously had a reason for arresting her!“

“You know that Sheriff Blake has had it out for her since she broke up with his cousin!“ I remind him.

“So, you’re saying it’s personal?“

“I think that’s a big part of it.”

“She threatened to kill him in front of a bunch of witnesses! After she vandalized his car,“ he remarks so loudly several people turn to look again.

“Keep your voice down!“ I chastise him.

“How are you going to tell Jake?“

“He already knows.“

“You told him? Without talking to me first?“

“No, the kids at school told him.“

“Great. Just great,“ he groans.

“Calm down. I’m sure it’s just a matter of time before we straighten this out. The police will figure out who the real killer is and Anne will be back home.“

“You better hope so,“ he grumbles.

We reluctantly walk toward the field together when Jake’s game starts. Thankfully, the phone rings, so I can excuse myself to take the call. I’m relieved it’s my cousin Harvey. Maybe Anne is out of jail already! Maybe they located the real killer! My heart thrums.

“Hey, Harvey! Please tell me this is good news.“

“It’s not.“

“All right, lay it on me.“

“The somewhat good news is that the bail hearing is first thing tomorrow morning, and the District Attorney promised me he would agree to let Anne out on her own recognizance, so no bail.“

“That’s a relief.“

“Yes.“

“Now what’s the bad news?“

“I have a contact in the medical examiner’s office who owed me a huge favor. Mind you, none of this has been released yet, but they know that Barney was killed by a blow to the head.“

“I kind of figured that, given the gash on his head,“ I tell him.

“Yes, well, they found your sister’s golf club stashed in the bushes in the backyard.“

He meets my burst of laughter with dead silence. “You *are* joking, right?” I ask.

“Noooo. What’s so funny?”

“My sister has never golfed a day in her life.” I laugh again with relief. This is all obviously just a huge misunderstanding and she’ll be out of jail by tomorrow at the latest. If not sooner!

“I don’t understand,” Harvey responds.

“What do you mean you don’t understand? My sister doesn’t golf. And she certainly doesn’t own any golf clubs. Phew, Harvey! I’ve been so stressed out, but obviously once Anne tells them she’s never set foot on a golf course, this whole thing will be done. You had me going there for a minute.”

“Molly, I don’t know how to break this to you, but the golf club head is inscribed with your sister’s name. It says Anne Simon right under the brand name.”

11

After a mostly sleepless night worrying about my sister, I take Jake to school before going to the courthouse for the bail hearing, which Harvey still assures me won't be a problem.

"Ask Aunt Anne what it was like to spend the night in the can."

"Can? Where did you pick up that word?"

"TV."

"You can ask her all about it when you see her."

"You think anyone tried to shank her?"

"Shank? Exactly what kind of TV are you watching?"

"Stuff." He shrugs.

Pressing my palm to my chest, I inhale sharply when I spot Anne and Harvey waiting inside Courtroom 12. She's disheveled and worn out but doesn't appear to have been shanked.

"How are you holding up, sis?"

"I'm okay. I'll be glad to get out of here. Harvey said he told you about the golf club."

"Yeah. But I don't get it. You don't golf. You hate golf."

“Oh yeah, I still hate golf!” She nods vigorously.

“So, what’s the problem? How did your name get on a golf club? There’s obviously some mistake here. Just tell the judge...” I trail off. Her expression tells me I don’t want to hear what she’s about to say.

“I told you, Barney gave me golf clubs for my birthday, even though I told him repeatedly that I hate golf.“

“I don’t remember that at all,” I protest.

“You were in the middle of your divorce drama at the time. You probably didn’t hear me.”

“Well, what did you do with them? Stuff them in a closet at home? Please tell me you donated them to charity.“

“I may have thrown them at him.“

“Thrown them? Did anyone see you?“

She nods reluctantly. “Pretty much everyone in his office.“

“But golf clubs are heavy. How could you throw them?“

“I didn’t say it was a good throw. Mostly they just flopped haphazardly onto the floor.“

“And then what?“

“I saw the office intern, Irene, smirking, and that’s when I knew.“

“Knew what?”

“I knew she picked them out. On purpose. I also knew something must be going on with them.“

“This still doesn’t tell me what happened to the golf clubs,“ I point out.

“How should I know? I stormed off.“

“Someone obviously took them and used one to kill Barney. We find the golf clubs, we find Barney’s killer.“

“So, you think it was someone from his office?“

“Do you know anyone who was mad enough to kill him?“

“Besides me?” she jokes.

"Don't say that!"

"Sorry, prison has hardened me."

"Hardy har. Now you sound like Jake."

"Okay, sorry, there was a guy named Collin."

"And?"

"They were competing for a huge promotion and agreed to keep it civil and not pull any dirty tricks. But Barney knew Collin had cheated on the CFA exam. Collin admitted it to him once in a weak moment. He obviously thought they were friends. They were friends until Barney wanted something. He told the higher-ups, and not only did Collin not get the promotion, but they also demoted him!"

"He must've been furious."

"He threatened to kill him!" Anne exclaims.

"In front of witnesses, I hope."

"In front of the entire office."

"Does he still work there?"

"As far as I know."

"Did they find any fingerprints on the club?" I ask Harvey.

"No."

"Well, there you go. How can they say that she did it if there were no fingerprints?"

"Because they're *her* golf clubs. She could've easily wiped off the fingerprints. Or worn gloves."

"Do we know when he died?" I ask, hoping somehow Anne has an alibi she forgot about.

"Around 9 AM yesterday."

"You were at work!" I exclaim.

"The shop is closed on Tuesdays, remember?"

Before I can ask her where she was, the judge appears.

"All rise for the Honorable Judge O'Malley."

Harvey shushes us while motioning for us to stand.

"Please be seated," the judge says.

I can barely see the leprechaun magistrate at first. He's so little he has to climb at least a dozen small stairs to reach the top of the bench. No one dare giggle at the tiny green man wielding an overly large gavel. First, he's the judge. Second, leprechauns possess powerful, dark magic.

One toe out of line and he'd be happy to curse any of us with a variety of maladies. I've heard stories about them cursing people that wrong them with horns, rashes, or extreme hair loss, just to name a few.

When the District Attorney stands, I instantly feel better. This will all be over shortly.

"Your Honor, the state requests $100,000 in bail."

Anne, Harvey, and I leap to our feet simultaneously, shouting, "What?"

"Order!" The judge scolds us. "I don't tolerate outbursts in my courtroom!"

"He lied!" I shout, jabbing my finger in the opposing attorney's direction.

"One more peep from you, and I'll remove you," the little green judge exclaims, wielding his gavel like a weapon.

"Sorry, Your Honor," I mumble.

Harvey tells me to sit down. He probably already regrets taking this case. "Your Honor, the DA swore to me yesterday that he'd ask for my client to be released on her recognizance. She has family here and is a small business owner. There's no reason to think she'd flee."

"Is this true? What's changed?" the judge asks the District Attorney.

"After further review of the case, Your Honor, I realized, given the high-profile nature of this case, that a costly bail is necessary."

"High profile meaning the Sheriff's cousin," I mutter.

The DA continues, "We've also come into some additional evidence this morning that we think is important."

"This is the first I'm hearing of it!" Harvey exclaims.

"I didn't have the chance to inform you. I just received this," the DA says.

"Yeah, right," I whisper while the judge glares at me. Yikes. I better watch it. The last thing Jake needs is a mom with horns.

"What is it?" the judge asks.

"Not only do we have an eyewitness who can place the defendant at the crime scene at the same time the victim was killed, we have a witness at the restaurant where she ate lunch afterward who says she showed up late and disheveled."

Harvey and I stare at Anne, who shrugs. "I've never set foot in the Baker place. There can't be an eyewitness. Someone is lying!" she hisses at us.

I've never seen Anne this pale. Not even when the principal of our high school caught her smoking behind the gym. She knows we'll need at least $10,000 cash, which we certainly don't have. Not easily, anyway. After that, I don't really hear what the judge says. What are we going to do? She can't just sit around in jail until we find the killer. She could get shanked!

"Where are we going to get that kind of money?" Anne turns to me the moment the judge leaves. When the bailiff comes to get her, I struggle to keep from bursting into tears.

"I know where we can get it," I announce loudly.

"Oh, Molly, are you sure you want to do that?" Anne asks.

"It's either that or you sit in jail."

"You know where you can get the money?" Harvey asks.

"Zach."

“Ah. Good luck with that.“ He grimaces.

“I’ll let you know how it goes,“ I assure them, hurrying from the courtroom. I can’t believe I have to beg my ex for money already. He’ll be thrilled.

“Molly, is everything okay with Jake?“ Zach asks, his face etched with worry when I march into his office.

“Huh? Oh, yes. Jake’s fine.“ It didn’t occur to me until just now that by showing up unannounced, he would automatically worry about Jake. I just thought it would be harder for him to turn me down in person.

“I need a huge favor,“ I tell him.

“Okay...“

Thankfully, Zach agrees, even if it’s reluctantly, to wire money to the bail bondsman. He knows Anne isn’t going anywhere, and he’ll get his money back. I’m sure the only reason he did it was so Jake won’t worry about his aunt. But it doesn’t matter. Whatever it takes to get Anne out of jail. Or the can as Jake would say.

Now that Anne’s bail is secured, I have a crime scene to break into.

12

My pulse racing, I park three houses away from the Baker house using several low-hanging trees for cover. A bead of sweat trickles down my back while I try to talk myself out of this crazy scheme.

I'm about to break into a crime scene. One that's still surrounded by painfully bright yellow "no trespassing" tape. I have to figure out who really killed Barney, for my sister's sake. But I can't mess this up by getting caught by the sheriff or filmed by a news reporter.

I need to get into the attic to see if it gives me any visions, or at least a sense of who was there when Barney died. Although I realize that even if I were to have a perfect vision of who really killed Barney, it will only help so much.

I can see it now. "Hi, Your Honor, I know my sister didn't do it because I snuck under the tape, broke into the house, and had a psychic vision that showed me it wasn't my sister." Nope. The best I can do is hope for some solid clues, then go out and prove it wasn't my sister.

My For Sale sign, still sitting proudly in the middle of the yard makes me cringe. How could it be that just yesterday I was so eager? Now it's embarrassing. They showed it on tv so many times last night I had to turn it off. I toy with the idea of taking it down, but that would just prove I was here again when I'm not supposed to be.

The next-door neighbor's house is quiet. Hopefully, they're at work. Where I wish I was. Making my way through their yard as stealthily as I can manage, someone calls out. "Hey you!" Oh great. Busted already.

I wrack my brain for a good excuse. Don't mind me, I'm just here admiring your tulips. Aren't spring flowers the best?

I make a bad criminal if that's the best excuse I can come up with. I should have brought Buster. That way, I could pretend he was lost. Who am I kidding? He'd just crawl into someone's hammock for a nap.

"Hey! I know you can hear me!" the voice shouts again.

When I realize it's a ghost calling to me from an open window I release an audible whoosh of air. It's an elderly man wearing pajamas. He must have died there in his sleep.

"Oh! Hello! If you don't mind, I'm kind of in a hurry," I tell him.

"That's what I told the sheriff's deputy yesterday."

Say what? "You talked to a deputy? What did you tell him?"

"I told him I saw a woman with long red hair and glasses hurrying away from the house. I insisted I only saw her briefly, but they were so excited when I gave them the description. Now I realize that was you!"

So, this is who told the Sheriff they saw my sister at the crime scene yesterday. We look so much alike anyway that people often mistake us for twins. If you only saw one of us from the back, you definitely wouldn't know which was which. Maybe I need a haircut.

But that answers the question of why a so-called eyewitness thought they saw my sister. Fat good that does me. "Hi, it's me again, Your Honor. While I was breaking into the crime scene, I talked to your eye witness. Turns out it was me he saw hurrying away. Not my sister."

"Did you see anyone else here yesterday?" I ask hopefully.

"Nope!"

"Okay, well, I have some business to attend to, so I have to be going."

"Come back again!" he shouts as I hurry away before someone hears us talking and calls the Sheriff.

There's only one way in that I can think of - other than breaking a window - which I'm not ready to do. Not yet anyway. The lockbox is still there. Yes! Please, please, please let the key be in here. Yes! It's there. My luck must be changing.

Before I sneak up the stairs, I glance out the picture window in front to make sure the coast is still clear. If I thought my pulse raced when I hid outside, that was nothing compared to what it's doing now. I'm almost afraid to go into the attic this time.

What if there's another body? I swear I'll run away as fast as I can and never tell a soul. I know, it's a horrible plan, but I can't handle another corpse right now. Or ever.

With each step the stairs creak unnaturally loud. They didn't do that yesterday did they? There's nothing but a large bloodstain on the floor. Yuck. That's bad enough. But still better than another victim.

I remind myself to calm down and get centered. No wonder I couldn't get a reading yesterday with all the shock and chaos. The calmer I am the easier it is to sense something. Yet despite my now chill demeanor I still get nothing. Not even the dark aura I felt yesterday on the stair steps. It's too late. Whatever visions I could have had are now gone.

What if I stood my ground and told Mr. Cabellos I had to touch the body? I may have learned the killer's true identity. But I wasn't willing to stand up to him, and I'll regret that forever. So many what if's. What if I refused to get Jake's soccer uniform? What if I left the restaurant instead of waiting an hour for my sister?

When the doorbell rings I let out a sharp yelp quickly clapping my hand against my mouth, hoping it wasn't as loud as I suspect. Will my ex pay for my bail too? What will Jake say when he finds out his mother got arrested?

The licensing board will never reinstate my license now. But I'm too busy to get shanked in prison! The doorbell rings again. Could I escape undetected out the attic window?

"Yoo hoo! Anyone home?" A woman calls out.

Huh? Since when does law enforcement say yoo hoo? I quietly inch my way down the stairs.

"Hello!" an older woman with gray hair and extra-large glasses exclaims when she sees me through the doorway. "I thought I saw someone in here! I'm Mrs. Kennets from across the street. There's been so much going on, I thought something else might've happened."

"Oh, hi there!" I tell her, trying my best to appear casual. "I'm the real estate agent. Just checking on things."

"Do you know how long they plan to keep all that yellow tape up?" she asks, letting herself in the door.

"No, unfortunately, I don't."

"It's so unsightly!"

Tell me about it! "You said you live across the street?"

"I sure do! 47 years next May. My Niles and I, God rest his soul, bought this place right after we got married. Ours was one of the first houses built here."

"Oh, that's nice, did you—

"—If you'll notice, the house next door has a garage, but it's only for one car. Back in those days, it was one car per family. Nowadays, everyone in the family has at least one. So many have two! Can you believe it..."

Oh, dear. I don't want to be selfish, but we really need to get out of here before the authorities show up. She has to stop talking at some point, right?

"...we couldn't afford the model with the garage. That's why we just have the carport..."

"I see." I nod along with her speech. If we get caught in the house because she has to give me the neighborhood history, I don't know what I'll do. Sure, I'm a real estate agent, and should be interested in this, but right now, I'm an agent with a suspended license, who's trespassing in a crime scene. Mrs. Kennets talks so fast that I'm convinced she hasn't inhaled once during this conversation.

"Mrs. Kennets, I don't mean to be rude, but do you recall seeing anyone here yesterday? Around 9 AM?"

"You mean that fellow who was killed here?"

"Yes! Did you see him here before that?"

"Mind you; I don't like to gossip. I don't think we should get involved in other people's business. Besides, if I say something, how can they promise me that they won't come after me later, you know? Best just to keep things to myself."

"Uh. Who will come after you?" I ask.

"The criminals! Or their friends!"

"Okay, but you think you saw the victim?"

"Yes." She nods.

"When was that?"

"You won't tell this to the police, right?"

"Not a word!" Unless it helps free my sister, of course.

"The guy they're showing on tv--"

"The victim."

"Yes, and another man were here yesterday before everything went haywire."

"What were they doing? Were they arguing? Could you tell?" My excitement grows. What if she saw something important?

"They didn't appear to be arguing. I don't know what they were doing. When I looked again, they were gone. Next thing I knew, I saw you with that vampire family. Then the Sheriff came. Did the vampires kill him? You have to be careful with them, you know."

"No, the vampires didn't kill him. He was dead when we arrived."

"Oh, I see. Do you think they'll buy the house?"

"Pretty sure the dead body killed that deal." I cringe at my unintentional pun.

"I suppose it would."

"What did the other man look like?" I press.

"He had medium brown hair, and he was about medium size. It was hard to get a good look. I didn't want them to catch me watching them. They might kill me next!"

"I wouldn't worry about that. I'm sure you're perfectly safe."

"I bet the young man who was killed thought that too!" she exclaims.

She has a point there. Now I at least know we should be looking for a medium size man with medium brown hair. Not a lot to go on, but better than nothing.

"I don't mean to be rude, Mrs. Kennets, but I must be going."

"Of course, dear. Next time you are here, do stop by, though. I'll play you a song on my ukulele."

"Your ukulele?"

"I play all the time for company. Everyone tells me it's delightful!"

I'm sure they do. Real estate could require more patience than I anticipated. How many stories will I have to listen to? Or ukelele solos?

Just as Mrs. Kennets and I finally move toward the door, a sheriff's deputy drives past the house slowly, like he's checking things out. If he comes back, we're in so much trouble.

"You know what? We should go through the backyard," I suggest, while shutting and locking the door.

"The backyard?"

"Yes."

"But why?"

"Because the sheriff's department just drove by; so, unless you want to repeat your story we need to go out of here."

"Let's go!" she says.

13

After I'm safely back in my car I get a text from Harvey.

Anne's bail has been posted. You can come get her now!

Thank goodness! My sister just spent the night in jail, accused of murdering her ex-fiancé. Never thought that would happen. We meet at the processing desk to wait for them to hand her the things she had on her when they arrested her.

"I assume you locked up my shop and made sure no one stole anything."

"Of course!"

"I can't wait to get a hot shower. Did you thank Zach for me?"

"I did."

"Does this mean I have to be nice to him now?" she asks, wincing at the thought.

"It couldn't hurt."

"He'll get his money back. It's not like I plan to take off or anything."

"I know who our so-called eyewitness is."

"Who? They must be lying because I swear to you, I've never set foot in the Baker house. Which means there's no way someone saw me there yesterday. Is someone trying to set me up?"

"They aren't lying. It was a ghost from next door. He saw *me* hurrying away from the house when I had to rush off to get Jake's uniform."

"Did you tell Harvey?"

"I texted him. I also talked to the neighbor across the street, Mrs. Kennets."

"You've had a busy morning! At this rate, you'll solve it in no time."

"Unfortunately, I don't think I've found out anything that's very useful. At least, not officially. She said she saw Barney and another man there right before he was killed.“

"That must be who killed him! Did she tell the police? Who did she see him with?“

"She claims she doesn't like to get involved. She's worried they'll come after her."

"Who's they?"

"I don't know."

"I'm confused." Anne scratches her head.

"I know. Bear with me. She said the other man had medium brown hair and a medium build."

"So, she just described half the guys in Melioras."

"It's all I've got so far. Do you know anyone else who hated Barney? You mentioned that guy from his office. Does that fit Collin's description?"

"It does!" she insists.

"We should pay Collin a visit right now. Do you think he's in the office?“

"Can I take a shower first? I feel like I've been trapped on an airplane for a week.“

"Fine. Take a shower and see if you can think of anyone else who hated Barney. I'll go to Collin. There's no time to lose."

After dropping Anne off at her house, three doors down from my own, I hightail it to Collin and Barney's office.

"Can I help you?" the receptionist asks.

"Is Collin in?"

"He is. Do you have an appointment?"

"No."

"I'm sorry, he only sees people by appointment."

"Tell him I'm here about Barney's murder."

Her eyes nearly bug out of her head. "One moment, please." She holds a finger up to me. "There's a woman here to see you," she says into the phone before lifting a questioning eyebrow at me.

"Molly Fitzle," I tell her.

"Molly Fitzle. She says she's here about..." she pauses like she just can't bring herself to say it. "Barney," she whispers his name. "He'll be right up," she says, using a business-like tone. Did she see my sister's golf club induced tantrum? I won't ask.

"Thank you." I tell her, stepping away from the desk, wiping my sweaty palms on my pants. Detective work is more nerve-racking than I realized.

What will I ask this Collin guy? "Hey, did you murder Barney?" What if he says, "I sure did!" How great would that be? I don't think it works like that. It certainly doesn't on TV. If it did, there wouldn't be a show. Meanwhile, I'm so busy daydreaming about how mysteries on TV are solved that I don't even see Collin approach.

"Molly Fitzle?" he asks, startling me out of my reverie.

"Oh! Yes, hi, Collin?" He fits the generic description, at least - medium build with medium brown hair. If he was 6 feet 4 inches and had long black hair, I'd probably turn around and walk out.

"Stacey said you were here about Barney? Are you with the police?"

“Erm, no, I just have some questions. Were you friends with Barney?“

While he pauses, I try to read him, but it’s murky at best. He’s searching for an answer he thinks I most want to hear. Finally, he settles on what feels like the truth. “We were friends once upon a time.“

“What happened?“

“Let’s just say we had a falling out.“

“Over a girl?“ I ask, not letting on how much I know.

He chuckles while shifting his feet. “No, it wasn’t over a girl. I foolishly admitted something to him in a weak moment, and he used it against me when we were competing for a promotion.“

“Did that make you angry?“

“I wasn’t happy if that’s what you’re asking.“

He may be maintaining his cool in front of me, but his anger is powerful. I sense it thrashing about inside of him. He’s definitely angry enough to kill.

“Did it make you angry enough to kill him? Because I wouldn’t blame you if it did.“ Perhaps the empathy card will get him to open up to me. If he could sense *my* emotions, he’d realize that I too was *almost* angry enough to kill Barney when we learned he was cheating on my sister. Emphasis on almost.

“No, I wasn’t angry enough to kill him.“ He adjusts his tie, shifting his feet again. “If you aren’t with the cops, why are you here? Who are you?“

“I’m here because a woman is unjustly accused of his murder, and I need to get to the bottom of it.“

“Hey, wait a minute, are you Anne’s sister?“

“I am.“ I raise my chin haughtily. No sense hiding it now.

“Then I don’t need to answer any of your questions.“

“Can you at least tell me where you were when Barney was killed?“

"I was at the Shady Pines Nursing Home visiting my pop pop. Not that I owe you any explanation. I mean, your sister is crazy, after all."

"My sister isn't crazy."

"How can you say that? Barney got her a set of premiere golf clubs. Those things were top of the line. But what did she do with them? Did she thank him for such a generous gift? No! She dumped them on the floor. She could have damaged them. We all saw it. Then she vandalized his car and threatened to kill him! You must know this already."

"I know *you* threatened to kill him in front of everyone in this office. I can feel your anger."

He falters, his facade crumbling. "If you're looking for Barney's enemies, you should talk to the intern he was messing around with. Irene. She comes in every afternoon at two."

14

Deep in thought, I head back to Anne's house, assuming she's ready by now. Collin could have killed Barney for sure. He's my number one suspect at this point. Okay, he's my only suspect, but still. He hated Barney. Now how do I prove he killed him?

He had his eye on those golf clubs. More than Anne anyway! He could have picked them up after she left when no one was looking. He has motive and means.

Plus, he was awfully quick to point to Irene, the office intern. Is he trying to throw me off his trail? Even though Mrs. Kennets insists she saw Barney with a man at the crime scene, which Collin wouldn't know, I'll follow up with her.

"Feeling better?" I ask my sister when she gets in the car smelling of soap and shampoo.

"Much! Did you talk to Collin? I thought of another suspect, by the way."

"I talked to Collin. He claimed he was visiting his pop pop at the nursing home when Barney was killed."

"Yikes. Would someone be evil enough to lie about visiting their grandpa in the nursing home, when they were really out killing someone? That's kind of the lowest of low, isn't it?"

"I would say the lowest of low would be the actual killing part, but I get where you're going with this. If he's telling the truth, I'll feel bad. You don't lie about things like visiting grandpa. That's just bad juju."

Did you get a reading from him?" she asks.

"Kind of. I could sense his anger toward Barney and it's extreme."

"Extreme enough to kill?"

"Yes."

"Any images?"

"Nope." I shake my head sadly. "Just the genuine emotion behind it all. He also insists the intern that you told me about could have killed him."

"But you said the neighbor said she saw him there with a guy. He's just saying that because we're closing in on him!"

"I agree. But I think we should talk to anyone who had even a remote possibility of killing Barney, so we can narrow it down from there. I mean, what if the intern was hiding in the house when the guy the neighbor saw lured him in?"

"Oh, that's a good point!"

"Who's the other person you think hated Barney enough to kill him?"

"Some golf pro at the Melioras Country Club. I think his name is Tyler," Anne says.

"What did Barney do to him?"

"Oh, you'll love this. Tyler had a thing for Irene—"

"—Irene's a popular gal."

"Don't even get me started! Anyway, he was madly in love with Irene forever and Barney knew it."

"Barney couldn't help himself and stole Irene away just for the thrill of the chase," I theorize.

"You got it, sister."

"Would he have access to the golf clubs though?"

"I don't know."

When we enter the swanky country club, the first thing we see is a large, colorful poster of a grinning elf. Picture Legolas with short brown hair and magnificent blue eyes.

Only I doubt *his* eyes change color. It's mesmerizing. There's a banner underneath highlighting his name along with a sales pitch to inquire at the front desk for lessons. The ladies at this club must eat it up.

"There it is. Tyler Cross." I point at the poster.

"Oh yeah, that's him." Anne nods knowingly. "Look, medium brown hair. Are his eyes really that blue in person? They're almost turquoise. I swear they could hypnotize me through the poster." Anne stares at it dumbfounded. She's not really hypnotized, is she?

"Good afternoon, ladies. Can I help you with something? Care for a lesson?"

Anne gapes at the extraordinary creature standing before us. Or is that me who's gaping? How could Irene pick Barney over this guy?

"We'd like to talk to you about Barney Mullins."

"I hope you're here to tell me he's dead," he responds with an eerily calm expression. Yet upon seeing our shocked reaction to that statement, he pales. "I was kidding! Okay, mostly. You aren't seriously here to tell me he's dead, are you?"

"You haven't heard? I thought by now everyone would know."

"You *are* serious. What happened?" he asks.

"He was murdered yesterday."

"Sakes alive, menuval!" he curses.

"Could you tell us where you were yesterday around 9 AM?"

"You don't seriously think I could have killed him, do you? I was joking when I said I hoped he was dead. I'd never kill anyone. I'm an elf, after all. We're peaceful creatures." He wiggles his pointy ears for emphasis. "We all but made up when he ordered those sweet customized clubs through me for his fiancé. I got a fat commission check from that. Although I've heard she's now his ex-fiancé so If I were you, I'd check her out…" he trails off, his previously cheerful expression fading when Anne's cheeks color. "Wait, are you Anne Simon?" he asks as she nods nervously. "Sorry about that. I tend to talk like that when I'm nervous."

"You still haven't told us where you were yesterday at around 9:00." I point out.

"What? Oh, yeah."

He reluctantly pulls his gaze away from my sister. Hang on a second. Is he actually flirting with her? At this time! When he catches me glaring at him, he at least has the decency to look embarrassed.

"I was giving a private lesson to Mrs. Robins on the back nine – the 16th hole to be exact. We were out there all morning." He holds his hand on the side of his mouth to whisper, "She really needs the lessons."

While I'm unable to read him - possibly because he's an elf – I'm sure he's lying about something. Which means we need to confirm his alibi with Mrs. Robins as soon as possible.

If Tyler is our killer, he won't get away with it.

15

After asking several of the staff at the country club, they tell us that Mrs. Robins isn't there, and they don't know when to expect her. But it's after 2:00 so we drive back to Barney's office to see if we can catch Irene.

"Hi again," I greet Stacey the receptionist. "I was told that Irene comes in at two?"

She glares at us. "They tell me if you showed up again, I'm supposed to call the authorities," she lectures us, snatching the phone from the console on her desk, rapidly punching in 911, but before she can say anything Anne reaches over the counter to press the disconnect button. She drops the phone, pushing herself away from the desk, her hands raised in surrender.

"I swear to you," Anne hisses, leaning over the desk so Stacey can hear her. "I didn't kill Barney and I'm not here to hurt you. I'm desperate. Someone who had access to the golf clubs Barney gave me, and someone who hated him more than me, killed him. I have to find out who before I go to jail for life for something I didn't do."

Have I mentioned my sister has a temper?

"Shouldn't you let the Sheriff figure that out?" Stacey snarks

"The Sheriff is convinced I did it. You know he's Barney's cousin. You must know he was no fan of mine so they aren't investigating this like they should. But he doesn't know Barney like I did. I'm begging you, just let me talk to Irene. I promise we aren't here to cause trouble. I just want to ask if she knows anything. If she could give us any clues."

"Fine, but don't tell anyone I let you in. I mean it," she insists, jabbing a finger in our direction. "I'm not losing my job over your problem."

"My lips are sealed." Anne motions across her mouth.

"I just saw her go into the break room. She always makes a cup of chamomile tea when she gets here."

"Thank you!" I exclaim as Anne strides purposefully down the hallway with me scrambling to keep up with her. Good thing she knows where the break room is.

When we get there, we find a young, pretty witch with long dark hair, and expressive green eyes. I sense that she's a spell witch, but I can't determine how powerful. When she sees Anne, she nearly drops the mug she's holding. I'm low-key worried she might curse us.

"You," she snarls.

"Yes, me," Anne snarls back.

Her eyes dart to the doorway in search of a quick exit, but I happen to be blocking it.

"I thought you were in jail."

"I was. Now I'm out," my sister says, moving toward her. Aside from the unfortunate outbursts my sister had where Barney is concerned, I swear she isn't a violent person. Even if she does have a temper. She's actually one of the most patient and gentle people I know.

There were days when Jake was a toddler and tried my patience so badly I wanted to tear my hair out. But Anne was always good with him. I think Barney just found a way to push every button she had.

They shouldn't have been engaged in the first place. Or even dating if I'm being perfectly honest.

"What do you want?" Irene continues to eye her nervously.

"I'm here about my fiancé."

"Don't you mean your ex-fiancé?" Irene grins cruelly.

"How soon after I broke up with him did he propose to *you*?"

Irene's grip tightens on the teacup. If she isn't careful that thing is going to shatter into a million pieces. I'm not getting anything from her but fear. But one doesn't have to be a psychic to get that. She's genuinely afraid of my sister. Maybe she thinks Anne really killed him.

"Oh, wait. He didn't propose to you, did he?" Anne presses. "I heard you broke up."

Irene slams the teacup onto the counter so hard some of it splashes out onto her hand. She jerks her hand back after getting burned. She then murmurs an incantation to heal the burn. Should I put myself between them? I'm worried about a catfight exploding.

I got between two fighting cats when I was a kid. That resulted in a trip to the ER for stitches and a tetanus shot. I still say it was worth it. At least the cats were okay!

"Admit it." Anne moves closer. "You were mad when he didn't propose to you after I left him. You were the one who talked him into giving me that ridiculous set of golf clubs for my birthday when I never showed even the slightest smidgen of interest in golf. You knew that I'd know you picked them out."

Irene edges away from Anne. But when she bumps against the water cooler, she gulps loudly. I almost feel sorry for her. She's obviously an impressionable young girl.

I'm sure Barney seemed so grown-up and cool. He had a great job, a nice house, and a fancy car. She probably loved the attention. She bought into the lies he told her.

When my sister broke up with him, I bet she thought that was her chance. But then he treated her poorly, as well.

“It was just a matter of time,“ she stutters. “He would’ve come around.“

“He was never going to marry you! Don’t you get that?” Anne points out, softening her stance just a bit.

“Now you sound like my brother, Gary. You didn’t know Baney like I did!” she shouts.

Then it happens. I get a vision. But it’s not what I expected.

“Do you know what happened to the golf clubs?” I ask.

“She threw them!“ she exclaims, pointing her finger at Anne.

“We know that. You’ve obviously both made mistakes here. Do you get that you have that in common? We just want to know what happened afterward. Who took the clubs?“ I ask her.

“How should I know?“

“Where were you when Barney was killed? What were you doing at 9 AM yesterday?” Anne barks at her.

“Not that it’s any of your business, but I was in class!“

“What’s going on here?“ a voice booms so loudly we all jump.

“They’re threatening me!“ Irene exclaims, dashing behind the Sheriff for safety

“Is this true? You were threatening her?“ The Sheriff plants his hands on his waist, glowering down at us.

“We did nothing of the sort,“ I explain.

“We just want to know where she was when Barney was killed. If she thinks we were threatening her, it’s because she has a guilty conscience,“ Anne adds.

“I don’t have a guilty conscience about anything. Barney and I were in love. She killed him because of it.“

“Then why didn’t he propose to you?“ Anne asks.

“All right, ladies. That’s enough!“ Sheriff Blake bellows.

I’m dismayed at the small crowd gathering in the doorway. This isn’t going at all the way I wanted it to.

“I’m here because we just received a hang up call to 911 from this office,” Sheriff Blake says.

Oops.

“Stacey tells me this is the second time you’ve been here today causing trouble. And you,“ he points at Anne, “are out on bail. If I take you in for disturbing the peace and trespassing, they’ll revoke it“

Oh dear, if we lose Zach’s bond money, Barney won’t be the only dead body in town this week.

“We were just leaving,“ I insist, grabbing my sister’s arm. When she opens her mouth to protest, I press my finger against her lips. “We’re done here!” I glare at her. “I'm not going to jail. Not today. Not ever.”

Pushing Anne out through the crowd is a challenge. “Excuse me. Pardon me,“ I plead. Why won’t these people move? “Please let us through,“ I beg. How humiliating.

16

Anne stops to catch her breath when we finally reach the sidewalk. “Why did you rush us out of there so fast? I had more questions!”

“You just wanted to yell at her some more. Do you really want to go back to the can?”

“Good point. What’s next?” she asks.

“We have to check out Irene’s brother, Gary.“

“Irene’s brother? Why on earth would we—“ She stops short when she sees my expression, her mouth falling open in shock. “You had a vision!”

“When she said, ‘you sound like my brother’ I saw a pair of handcuffs.”

“What does that mean? Oh my gosh, does it mean that he killed Barney and you see him getting arrested for it?” Anne exclaims, hopping up and down with glee.

“You know it doesn’t work exactly like that,” I tell her, placing my hands on her shoulders to stop her from jumping. “I get the sense that it was in the past. It’s worth checking into, regardless.“

“So how do we do that? Just walk up to the brother and ask him if he’s ever been arrested?”

“No silly, those records are online.“

“I don’t want that kind of search showing up on my phone, though,” she insists.

“Paranoid much?“

“Possibly. I just don’t think it will hurt to be extra cautious right now.“

“Then let’s try the library,” I suggest.

“The library? They have internet there?“

“I think so. All those people staring at computers are staring at something.“

The library is small, but it will get the job done. There’s a librarian keeping watch over the computers. She’s a tiny fairy, with a harsh look about her. She glares at us when we walk in as if she was anticipating trouble. If only she really knew!

“How does this work?“ Anne asks a little too loudly as we pull chairs in front of the only open monitor in this row.

“Shush!“ a vampire says with his fingers to his lips. We’re delighting people wherever we go today.

“Remember, you’re in a library,“ the fairy scolds us.

I hold up my hands in innocence, then place a finger against my lips. We get it, soft whispers only. After several minutes of searching, we find the portal where they keep the public police records.

Anne repeatedly glances behind us, as if someone will sneak up on us, and know exactly what we’re doing and why. Unfortunately, this only makes the librarian more suspicious of us. We enter Gary’s name, and his arrest record pops up.

Right in front of our eyes is official proof. Shortly before his murder, Barney took out a restraining order against Gary.

“This proves it!“ Anne announces in a stage whisper, which still isn’t quite enough for some library patrons who shush us again.

“Don’t get us kicked out of another place today,“ I hiss at her.

When we dig deeper through the records we learn the arrest was only a month ago. Barney and Gary got into a fight at the bar where Gary works. It doesn't have very many details other than the arrest. The following day Barney filed for a restraining order.

Anne pokes her finger loudly against the monitor, once again earning us unwanted attention from the librarian. According to his mugshot, Gary is medium build with medium brown hair.

"This guy literally came to blows with Barney over his sister!"

"Ladies!" the librarian chastises us. "This is my last warning."

"We should print this out! How do we do that?" Anne asks me.

"I'm not sure. Ask the librarian."

"You ask the librarian. She scares me."

"Hey, you were the one who got arrested," I point out.

"That's just rude."

"But true!"

"Excuse me!" the librarian exclaims pointing at the door.

"We need to print out a few pages, and then I promise we're leaving," I assure her.

We head immediately to the Partying Pony Bar even though I insist it won't be open in the middle of the afternoon, Anne tells me it will. "Where else do the unemployed, sad people go?"

She's right. The bar is open. We squint our eyes to adjust to the dim light after being out in the bright afternoon sun. There's just a handful of people here, most tucked into dark corners nursing a drink, avoiding the sunlight peeking in through the slats of the window shades. It smells like stale beer and pretzels with an undercurrent of loneliness and depression. I know. So cliché. It is a bar after all.

Gary is entertaining the lone man at the bar with his perfect imitation of Bert and Ernie from Sesame Street.

"How does he do that?" Anne marvels.

"He's a mutatio demon. They're known for their chameleon-like abilities. The older, more gifted ones can change their outward appearance. Most just imitate voices or physical characteristics."

"Can they do magic?"

"No, but they're incredibly strong and agile."

“Strong enough to kill someone with a golf club?”

“Definitely.”

“What can I get for you ladies?“ Gary asks when we slide onto stools at the bar. He’s medium build with medium brown hair just like his mug shot.

“What do you have on tap?“ I ask.

“I have a golden wheat beer I just tapped,” he says.

“Bourbon. Neat,“ my sister requests.

“What?” She shrugs when my head snaps around in her direction. “You’re driving.“

“It’s been a long week,“ I explain to Gary.

While he prepares our order, Anne pulls a small bowl of pretzels toward us.

“What brings you in today?” Gary asks. “You’re not part of the usual crowd.“

“We came to see you,“ my sister says before I can make up a good story.

“Me?“

“Yeah, are you Irene’s brother?“

“Who wants to know?“

"I was engaged to Barney."

"Ah, you're the fiancé," he says, cringing.

She nods. "Former fiancé, to be exact."

"You aren't here to cause trouble, are you? I'm sorry my sister did what she did. I warned her over and over to stay away from that loser. I told her he'd never leave you."

"Then I left him. And now he's dead."

"Is it true? Did you kill him?" he asks.

How can they both be discussing this so matter-of-factly?

"I didn't," she answers, tossing another pretzel in her mouth.

"I wouldn't blame you if you did. I admit it certainly crossed my mind," he admits.

"We know he filed a restraining order against you," I tell him. "What happened?"

"We got into a shoving match," he says pinching his lips in disgust, "and I took a swing at him, but that was all it amounted to. I didn't even break anything. But the deputies hauled me down to jail because of course he's related to the sheriff. My boss was furious. But I didn't even have to spend the night in jail. Then the process server shows up the next day with a temporary restraining order. I almost lost my job because of that jerk."

He isn't lying. But like everyone else we've talked to I can feel the anger roiling inside him.

"That guy was a piece of work. Seduces my young sister with empty promises, then comes here, picks a fight, and takes me to court over nothing. I'm serious when I say I wouldn't blame you if you did kill him. I'll never know what you or my sister saw in him."

"There are days when I wonder that myself," Anne responds. "And, not for nothing, but he brought out the worst in me too."

He pours her another shot of bourbon. "On the house."

Anne raises her glass to him while I glare at her. That's all I need is a drunk sister to escort around.

"Where were you when Barney was killed?" I ask.

"Are you saying you think I killed him?"

"We're just trying to rule out all the people who hated him, that's all."

"I was an hour away in Tenebris Village at the Swift Auction House picking up some expensive scotch my boss won in an auction. You can ask him if you want." ￼￼

"Uh oh." Anne taps frantically on my arm.

"What now?" I ask following her finger to the window. It's Sheriff Blake!

17

"Thank you for your hospitality, but we have to go!" I insist.

"Don't you want to talk to my boss?" he asks.

"Some other time. Hey, is there a back door we could use?"

"You can go out that way, I guess." He hesitates before pointing to a door marked "Employees Only."

"Thanks!" we exclaim in unison, hurrying away before the Sheriff catches us again.

"Phew! That was a close one." This sneaking out the back door habit gets old fast.

"You know Gary will tell him we were there," Anne points out while we lean against the alley wall to catch our breath.

The course brick digs into my back; I wrinkle my nose in disgust at the smell of trash and spilled liquor. "I know; we'll just have to deal with that later. But if we don't leave now, we'll be late picking up Jake from school. And I do not need to hear from Zach again about how I'm being a negligent parent."

"Hey, Aunt Anne, how was your night in the clink?" Jake asks, sliding into the backseat of the car.

"It sucked. Never get arrested. Stay in school. Don't do drugs. Blah, blah, blah."

"I'll keep that in mind," he laughs.

"How was school?"

"It was okay. Some of the kids were messing with me about having an aunt who's a murderer."

"What?" I exclaim. "The kids are picking on you?"

"Not all of them. Just the usual ones who are jerks to everyone."

"I'm talking to the principal right now!" I insist, car tires squealing as I execute a sharp u-turn in the middle of the street to return to the school pickup zone. When a driver honks angrily at my about-face, I wave my hand dismissively, although that time, it was definitely my fault.

"Don't you dare!" Jake protests. "If they find out my mommy ratted them out, they'll never back off. I got it handled. School is kind of like the prison yard, right, Aunt Anne?"

"I was only in there for a night!"

"Whatever. Did anyone try to shank you?"

"No, no one tried to shank me! You?"

"Nah, not yet."

"Kids don't really get shanked at his school, do they?" she asks me.

"No. But I obviously don't supervise his TV time enough."

"So, what did you guys do all day?" Jake asks.

"After we got your aunt out of the slammer, we looked into some suspects."

"Cool. You coming over for dinner, Aunt Anne?"

"I don't know; what are you having?"

"Tacos."

"Oh, I'm definitely coming to dinner."

"Dinner is at 5:00 sharp. Don't be late!" Jake scolds her when she gets out of the car in front of her house.

"You got it!" she shakes her head, laughing.

"You think she'll be on time?" I ask him.

"Not a chance."

"Hi, Buster!" Jake exclaims happily, dumping his things in the doorway, which I nearly trip over.

Jake! My boy! I'm so happy to see you. You've been gone forever.

"What did you do today?" he asks, wrapping his arms around Buster in a big hug.

I took 11 naps, ate some kibble, drank water, oh, you'll love this, I yelled at three squirrels to get off my lawn!

"C'mon boy, let's go outside and throw the ball."

Woo hoo! Best day ever!

"Jake, pick up your..." I call out to his retreating back. Why do I even bother?

"Back in my day my mother would take a switch to my backside for that kind of disrespect," Oliver tells me.

"You don't say?" I respond absentmindedly.

"Assuming you get your real estate license back he'll have to start minding. He needs to pull his weight around here."

"He's ten," I remind him. "What do you think he should do? Quit school and get a job?"

"He could start with picking up after himself. How hard is it to require him to put his things away before he goes out to play?"

"I know, I know," I respond, blowing my bangs up out of my eyes in exasperation while I put Jake's school things away. "I plan to talk to him once I get this mess with Anne straightened out. Hey, wait a second. How did you know they suspended my license?"

"The ghost community talks."

"Does the ghost community know who killed Barney?"

"That part I don't know, but I can tell you it doesn't look good for Anne at all. Sheriff Blake is on the war path. A ghost in the Sheriff's Department told me he overheard him telling a deputy that he would make Anne pay if it was the last thing he did."

"I knew it! I knew this was personal. If you hear anything else let me know, okay?"

"So now you're telling me I'm useful?" he asks.

"Don't get carried away."

"You're here early!" I greet my sister at the door in shock.

"Check this out," she insists, pushing through the door without so much as a hello. "I put together a list of suspects and what we've learned so far," she says proudly, brandishing her iPad.

"Wow! So organized!"

"Hey, dad!" Jake tells his dad who arrives about three seconds after Anne.

Anne looks at me questioningly, so I shrug. "Jake invited him too," I mouth at her.

“Hey, there, kiddo. How’s it going?“

“Aunt Anne spent the night in the can!“

“So I heard,“ Zach says.

“Come to check on your money?“ Anne asks.

“Something like that.“

“Thank you for the bail money,“ Anne says swallowing loudly. This is painful for her.

“You’re welcome.“ Zach nods.

Painful for both of them!

“Just so you know,” I take Zach aside in the kitchen when Jake returns to his video game, “Jake mentioned some kids at school were hassling him about Anne getting arrested.“

“Did you go to the principal?“

“I tried, but he insisted that would cause more problems than it would solve.“

“He’s ten years old! What does he know? I don’t like this one bit. Maybe he should stay with me until this is all over.“

“No!“ I respond sharply. “He’s fine where he is. If the kids at school cause too much trouble, we’ll deal with it. Besides, I plan to solve this sooner rather than later.“

Oops. Why did I just admit that?

“What do you mean, *solve this*? You’re a real estate agent, not a private investigator. Please tell me you’re not investigating this.” When he sees the expression on mine and Anne’s faces, he gets mad. “Oh no, what are you two up to now? Don’t you have a new job to concentrate on?“ he points at me.

Drat. Why did I open this can of worms? “The real estate board suspended my license.“

“You’ve only had it for a day!“ he exclaims.

“Yeah, tell me about it.“

"So, now you think you can figure out who really killed Barney on your own?"

"Kind of," I tell him wiggling my hand.

"This is dangerous. You need to leave this to the sheriff."

"The sheriff has a personal vendetta against Anne. Oliver even confirmed it this afternoon. Remember, Barney is his cousin," I point out defensively.

"So that's what you did all day. Investigate Barney's murder?"

"Aside from losing my brand new real estate license, yes."

"You didn't lose it, it's just on hold," Anne reminds me.

"I'm sure I'll regret asking this, but did you learn anything useful?" Zach asks.

"Oh! Oh! Can I show him what I've put together?" Anne begs.

"The cat's already out of the bag, so you might as well."

Anne shows him what she's done so far, and I have to admit it's quite impressive. She has photos of Collin, Irene, Tyler, and Gary. Each photo has a column of notes next to it.

"Why does that one look like a mug shot?" Zach asks.

"Because it is," we respond in stereo.

"Great."

"When we were talking to his sister--"

"--who's his sister?" Zach interrupts.

"The tramp Barney cheated on me with."

"Did you know that this Gary guy had a record *before* you talked to him?" Zach demands.

"Of course! When Irene told us that we sounded like her brother, Molly had a vision of handcuffs..."

How does Anne not see me signaling at her to shut up?

"...so we went to the library, oh, but not before the Sheriff threw us out of Barney's office. We looked up the arrest records and saw that he was arrested for fighting with Barney who then filed a restraining order against him."

Anne falters when she sees the look of disdain on Zach's face and finally notices I'm trying to get her to stop talking.

"I think dinner is almost ready!" I announce.

"Wait! Sheriff Blake is here!" Oliver the poltergeist announces.

"Are you serious?"

"Is he following us or what?" Anne asks.

Buster's bark booms loudly when the doorbell rings.

Someone is at the door, you guys! Hurry!

"Sheriff." I nod, reluctantly opening the door.

"May I come in?" he asks, his voice gruff with resentment.

"Of course."

I open the door wide, watching as he ducks to clear the doorway. "Good, you're all here," he says scanning the room with a bitter look.

Buster approaches him like he does all company, giving him a gentle sniff. When he realizes who it is, however, he lets out a bizarre squeaking noise before taking off up the stairs.

There's a werewolf in the house! Run for your lives!

"I hope you've come to tell us you caught Barney's killer," I tell him.

"I've come to ask why I'm hearing reports that you two are going around town asking people where they were when Barney was killed."

"What are *you* doing to find the *real* killer?" I ask with more bravado than I actually feel. "If you ask me, you should be out there searching for the rest of the golf clubs!"

"I didn't ask you," he growls.

"We have every right to clear my name!" Anne tells him defiantly.

"You *don't* have every right to interfere in my investigation. Especially when you're still my primary suspect. This is my last warning. Stay out of my way or else."

"Or else what?" Anne says.

"Or else I'll make sure that your bail is revoked," he says, staring icily at Zach because he obviously knows Zach provided the bond money. "And you'll be taken into custody until trial."

18

With my real estate career temporarily on hold, I agree to help Anne in her crystal and potions shop. She considered closing it until we figure out who killed Barney, but decided that would be bad for business.

I didn't think that people would visit the shop of an accused murderer, but I didn't tell her that. Turns out the most popular crystal and potions shop in town still does plenty of business, even when the owner is a murder suspect.

"Hey, what's up?" I ask Zach when he calls, knowing it shouldn't be a Jake emergency because the school would call me first, but it still makes me nervous.

"You won't believe this but I just saw that Gary guy leaving a pawn shop here."

"What do you mean here? Where are you?"

"I'm in my office in Aletera Porta. I was getting a bagel at the bakery when I saw him leaving the pawn shop. He was acting really sketchy, so I went in, after he drove away to see what he was up to."

"Did they tell you?"

"Yes. The owner said he sold him a Rolex watch."

"A Rolex? What was Gary doing with a Rolex?"

"I don't know, but it just seems off to me. The owner said he checked it against the stolen goods database, but it didn't come up."

"You're sure it was him?"

"It matches the guy you showed me last night on Anne's iPad."

"I'm still not convinced this is suspicious," I admit.

"Just do me a favor and ask Anne if Barney had a Rolex."

"Okay, fine. Hey Anne, did Barney have a Rolex?"

"Oh, yeah. He loved that watch more than anything. It was the first big purchase he ever made."

"Uhhh, Zach just saw Gary pawning a Rolex in Aletera Porta."

"No way! Do you think it was Barney's watch? What if he killed him, then took it?"

My heart races, just thinking that we could have actual proof Gary killed Barney. "It's worth driving to the pawn shop to investigate. You'd know Barney's watch if you saw it, wouldn't you?"

"Yes! He had it inscribed to himself, from himself, if you can believe it."

"Yes, actually, I can believe that!"

"Should we call the Sheriff first?" she asks.

"First, we should confirm that it's Barney's. Then we'll call the Sheriff. If we send him out on a wild goose chase, he'll lock us up and throw away the key just for spite."

"Then what are we waiting for?"

"We should close up your shop first," I suggest, pointing to several customers who are in line, waiting to pay.

It takes longer than I anticipated to finish with the remaining customers in Anne's shop. By the time we arrive at the pawn shop in Aletera Porta Village I feel like I chugged a pot of coffee and have caffeine jitters. This could be our big break!

"Okay, be cool," Anne tells me when we arrive.

"Me? You're the one who loses her temper and throws golf clubs at people."

"I told you, it was more like *dropped* the golf clubs. Only in a big and dramatic way."

"Whatever. Just you be cool yourself."

"Excuse me," I say to the tall, thin man behind the counter, who's carefully examining a sparkling engagement ring. I guess that didn't go as planned. I should ask Anne about hers sometime. "I'm told you bought a Rolex watch from someone this morning?"

"Yeah," he grunts. "What of it?" he asks, pausing to stare at me through his magnifying glasses. "Why is everyone so interested in that dang watch?"

"I know this sounds like a weird request, but could we see it?" I ask, hopefully.

"Nope."

"Um. Why not?"

"I already sold it to a collector. You interested in a Rolex? Or did you lose one? Cuz if you did, I checked it against the database, and it ain't been reported."

"Can you tell us who you sold it to?"

"You the cops?"

"Nope."

"I sell a lot of high-end stuff to the collector, who sells them overseas."

"Do you have his contact information?"

"No."

"How do you normally get in touch with him?"

"I don't. He just stops by sometimes to see what I have. I don't ask questions. You sure you ain't the cops?"

"We're sure. Is this the guy who sold you the watch?" I ask, showing him a picture of Gary.

"Yep. That's him. Seriously, what's the deal with this watch? I gotta say, you're making me nervous."

"We think he took it off a murder victim."

"And, we're done here," he says, throwing his hands in the air. "I ain't got nothing to do with none of that."

"Could you at least do me a favor?"

"Do I look like I'm in the mood to do any favors?"

"If he tries to pawn anything else, can you call me before you do anything with it?" I beg, handing him my card.

"What else does he need to sell?"

"I'm not sure. Maybe some golf clubs."

"Says here you're a real estate agent."

"I am. I was. I am."

"Well, are you or ain't you?"

"She's on temporary leave!" Anne says.

"I I don't know, I'll think about it. But don't get your hopes up. He ain't one of my regulars, so I don't expect to see him again. If you want golf clubs, I got plenty," he insists, pointing to the corner.

"It's a very specific set of clubs," I explain.

"Like a special brand or what? You sure talk in circles."

"They're inscribed with my name," Anne says. "Anne Simon."

"He stole your golf clubs?"

"No. It's just that. Never mind, it's a long story. Could you just call us if he comes in here again."

"I'm tellin' you, I don't want no trouble here."

"We're not trying to cause trouble sir, I promise you."

The begrudging exhalation that follows, tells me he's just about out of patience. "If you ladies ain't buying nothin', I have paying customers I gotta help," he says, nodding toward the eager couple at the end of the counter. Maybe they'll buy the engagement ring.

"We're sorry to have bothered you. Thank you for your time," I tell him, steering Anne out the door when she opens her mouth to protest. At least we can leave by the front door this time.

19

"I know you won't like this, but I think we need to tell Sheriff Blake what we just learned," I tell Anne.

"I agree."

"Really?"

"Really. How else could Gary get Barney's watch unless he killed him?" she points out. "I know the sheriff doesn't like me, but even he'll have to see the logic in this. You know what? I'm so convinced we've found the killer, I'll even drive us there."

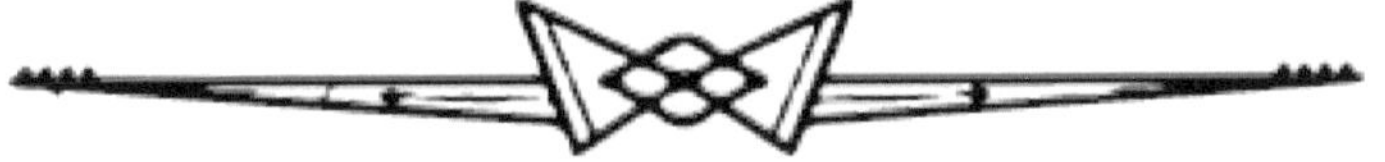

"It must be my lucky day! You're here to confess?" Sheriff Blake says after we persuade the desk sergeant to let us meet with him.

"No, but we have information we know you'll want."

"Do tell. And how did you come up with this so-called information?" he asks planting his elbows on his desk while staring at us intensely. I take a deep breath and close my eyes. The flashback to his warning from just last night sends a chill down my spine.

I forgot about that already when I got so excited over Zach's phone call. Still, what we have to say is important. Surely, he won't be mad when we tell him? As Anne already pointed out, he can't dismiss the logic here.

"Gary killed Barney!" Anne announces before I can formulate a good story.

"You know this, how?" has asks, still skeptical.

"Well, uh," Anne responds nervously, "we found out that Gary sold Barney's Rolex watch to a pawn shop in Aletera Porta Village this morning!"

For a moment, I'm certain he's considering what this could mean. This is exciting. Anne is on the verge of becoming a free woman.

"*Again*, how do you know this?" he asks.

Uh oh. He's getting impatient, but we can't exactly tell him everything. If we get Zach in trouble, he'll be furious. "We saw him," I offer before Anne can slip up, exposing Zach.

"You *saw* him sell this watch that supposedly belonged to Barney?"

"No, we saw him leaving the pawn shop." Oh dear, my nose must be growing.

"Then how do you know he sold *Barney's* Rolex?"

"We asked the guy who owns the place!" Anne says.

When he sits up straight, like he's actually interested in what we're saying, I congratulate myself for suggesting we do this. Anne's exoneration is just moments away.

"He showed you the watch. You know it's Barney's Rolex?"

Way to burst my bubble. "No, we didn't exactly see it," I mumble.

"Why not?"

"He already sold it to someone else by the time we got there," Anne responds, jumping when I kick her foot under the chair. She's a horrible liar.

"Now I'm confused," Sheriff Blake says, when he obviously isn't. He knows he caught us in a lie. "You saw him leave the pawn shop, but it took you 'so long' to get there," he emphasizes using air quotes, "that he'd already sold the watch, which you claim is Barney's, so you never actually saw the watch."

The watch has to belong to Barney, but without solid proof, we're no better off than when we started this morning. At least not where the Sheriff is concerned.

"Correct me if I'm wrong," he says menacingly, "but wasn't it just last night that I warned you to stay out of my investigation?"

Gulp.

"Now I can revoke your bail," he jabs an accusatory finger at Anne, "and I can book you as well. Or you can get out of my sight and let me do my job. Which would you prefer?"

"We were just leaving!" I assure him, pulling Anne to her feet before she says anything that will get us in trouble.

"Why does this keep happening to us?" my sister whines as I quickly usher her down the hallway and out through the lobby.

"I don't know, but since Sheriff Blake refuses to take this seriously, we'll have to confront Gary ourselves."

"Are you sure that's safe?"

"What other choice do we have?" I remind her.

"All right, Partying Pony, here we come. I wonder if I can get another free shot?"

"You better hope he doesn't actually shoot *at* us this time!"

"Way to reassure me, sis."

"Hey, ladies. Back again?"

"We have a question for you," Anne says.

"Okay. Right to the point. I appreciate that," he responds charmingly.

"Did you sell Barney's Rolex to a pawn shop?"

In a flash, charming Gary isn't so charming. He tilts his head at us, like he's pondering how he should respond. When he slams his hands on the bar top, glaring at us threateningly, we back up. "I know my rights. I don't have to tell you anything. You're working for the cops, aren't you?"

"Of course we aren't, but unless you have a good explanation about Barney's watch, we'll report you to the cops," I threaten.

I consider telling Anne to run, when he stares us down. What if he leaps over the bar to come after us? Maybe this wasn't such a great idea after all.

"All right, all right, I admit it!" he shouts, throwing his hands in the air, his face sagging in defeat.

Is it just me, or is he about to confess?

"My stupid sister took his watch."

"Irene took the watch?" I respond in shock.

"After *you* killed him!" Anne shouts, her face glowing triumphantly.

"What? Killed him? No! Of course not!" he insists.

"But you just admitted you know she took his watch," I point out.

"She took his watch two weeks ago - to teach him a lesson - she said. Snuck into his house while he was at work because she still had a key. She claimed he loved that watch more than her."

Anne nods knowingly.

"She wanted him to call her and ask if she had it. I don't know why. Maybe she was hoping they could meet up and she could convince him they belong together. Who knows? People do stupid stuff for love, you know."

Anne nods again.

As preposterous as his story sounds, my reading tells me he isn't lying. What a disappointment.

"That still doesn't explain why you sold it to the pawn shop," I point out. "It wasn't yours to sell."

"After you found his body, she realized how it would look if the authorities caught her with the watch, so she begged me to help her get rid of it before anyone found out about it. I told her just to take it back to the house and leave it, but she insisted a nosy neighbor might see her and call the cops. Then she wanted to throw it in the lake, but I told her that was even dumber than her stealing it in the first place. Do you know what those things are worth?"

"So you offered to sell it for her. You thought if you did it in a different village, no one would know you."

"Exactly. I know it was stupid, but, family you know. What are you going to do?"

I glance at Anne, who stares at the floor as if she's discovered a fascinating bug.

"I hear you," I tell him, shaking my head in disappointment.

"Did you get anything?" Anne asks me after we leave.

"He isn't lying."

"Well, phooey. The entire time we were there, I was sure you were sensing a lie. I was getting excited about catching the real killer."

"Nope. All I got was truth."

"So, we're back to square one. Or at least back to investigating the other suspects."

"I'm afraid so," I tell her.

As we start to trudge back to Anne's car, utterly defeated, my mind awhirl with thoughts of who could have killed Barney, we hear arguing in the alley behind the bar. Anne grabs my arm to pull me back against the wall, her finger to her lips, warning me not to make any noise.

When we peek around the corner to see what all the commotion is about, I gasp softly. It's Gary and some other man. Gary is smoking so he must be on a break. But who is the other guy and why are they arguing?

"I just got a call from the auction house," the man says, "they want to know when you're picking up the scotch that I won. I thought you were going to get it up days ago."

"Sorry about that, boss. I got sidetracked and didn't make it up there."

"I want my scotch! I'm hosting a party this weekend and if I don't have that to show off to my guests, my wife will pitch a fit."

Anne and I stare at each other unmoving and openmouthed.

Gary lied to us about where he was when Barney was killed!

20

"I know this will sound crazy," I tell Anne after we hurry back to her car, hoping Gary didn't see us lurking near the alley.

"I know exactly what you're about to say, and I want no part of it!" she protests.

"But what else can we do?"

"Send an anonymous note?"

"Like Sheriff Blake will believe that!" I scoff.

"You think he'll believe you when you show up a second time after he already threatened to arrest both of us like an hour ago?"

"I get all of that, but c'mon, we know Gary sold Barney's watch *and* lied about his alibi. I'm sure I can convince the sheriff to listen to us now."

"I'm sorry, Molly, but I refuse to set foot in that place again. Not voluntarily, anyway. I'll drop you off if you want me to, but then I'm going home. For the record, I still say an anonymous note is the best way to go. I have a bad feeling about this."

"All right, fine, give me a ride to the Sheriff's Department. You can thank me after they drop the charges against you."

"Hello. I'm here to see Sheriff Blake," I tell the desk sergeant for the second time this afternoon.

"Didn't he just throw you out of here?"

"Well, I wouldn't exactly say he threw me out..."

"Then what *would* you say?"

"I have more evidence," I insist.

"About?"

"About the murder of Barney Mullins."

"Ms. Fitzle." Is it just me, or did the sheriff growl when he said that? "I can only assume you're here because you *want* to go to jail?"

"Just give me two minutes of your time. Please? I swear I have more information that's relevant to the case."

"Information that you got investigating the murder when I've repeatedly told you to stop."

"Um, yes?" I know, I know, I'm on fragile ice here, but if I can just persuade him to at least consider the possibility, it will be worth it. If I get arrested, they have to let me make a phone call. I can tell Zach to pick up Jake from school and feed Buster. Spending a night or two in jail will be worth it if I can somehow plant a seed in the Sheriff's mind.

"I don't know why I'm even agreeing to this, but a night in jail may convince you to stop this nonsense. You've got one minute. Go."

"But I asked for two minutes," I foolishly point out.

"45 seconds," he says, glancing at his watch.

"Okay, okay!" I quickly point out everything we've learned so far about Gary. "He got arrested for fighting with Barney, who then took out a restraining order against him."

"If that's all you've got, you can save it. We obviously already know that. It still doesn't point to murder."

"Then he sold Barney's watch in a pawn shop in Aletera Porta."

"You told me that already, and I reminded you that you have no actual proof of this. Deputy Hart! Please escort Ms. Fitzle to lockup. She's spending the night with us."

"Wait! Wait! I have one more thing!" I plead while the deputy takes my arm, ready to lead me to a jail cell. This is scarier than I thought it was going to be. "Gary lied to us about where he was when Barney was murdered."

"Assuming I'm taking any of this seriously, which I'm not, how did Gary get one of your sister's golf clubs?"

"I don't know," I whisper. That's one part I still can't answer. If only she hadn't left the golf clubs lying on the floor in Barney's office. We just don't know where they went after that.

Sheriff Blake nods at Deputy Hart, who starts to lead me away once again. I've really blown it this time. Zach will be furious, and I've just made Anne look guiltier than ever. Anne had the right idea. I should have just gone home and sent an anonymous letter.

"Sheriff, there's a call on line one you need to take," the desk sergeant tells him.

"Hold up a sec," he tells the deputy. "This better be good," he says to the sergeant.

"It is."

"Sheriff here," he says, after picking up the phone at the front desk. "What? Are you sure?" He stares at me so intently my stomach roils. I don't need to be clairvoyant to know this is about to go south. His expression says it all. "Okay, thank you very much."

"A witness," he tells me, "just saw Gary get run down by a car that matches your sister's car. He fell into a ravine and was seriously injured. So much for your Gary killed Barney theory."

The floor tilts underneath me I'm so horrified. When my knees buckle, Deputy Hart pulls me up.

"Here's a piece of advice for you." Sheriff Blake moves in close and this time I know he growled. "You better find your sister before I do. It would be best for everyone involved if she turns herself in. And consider her bail revoked."

21

My sister is back in jail this morning, not only suspected of murdering Barney but also for attempting to kill Gary. I still don't know what to think, other than I know she didn't do either. Harvey tells me the witness who reported it said she saw Gary jogging when a light-colored car with heavily tinted windows purposely swerved at him.

The witness is so upset she can't remember if the car was white, gray, or silver and didn't get a license plate. But she thinks she remembers seeing the letter N on the car. Was it a bumper sticker? A logo? She doesn't know. And she can't even be certain she saw a letter.

The light-colored car description only applies to most of the cars in Melioras. Just the other day at the grocery store, Jake pointed out that nearly every vehicle in the parking lot was white, gray, or silver. He was right. It's clearly a common color. But that's useless to us at this point. Unfortunately, my sister also drives a silver sedan, which Sheriff Blake was happy to point out made her look guilty.

The car didn't actually hit Gary. It was a narrow miss, but he fell into a ravine when he leaped from its path. If the witness hadn't seen it, who knows how long he would have been there? When I asked what this had to do with my sister supposedly killing Barney, Sheriff Blake insisted this was all too much of a coincidence not to be related.

Even though Anne swears she was home when it happened, they don't believe her. The deputies who came to question her noticed her car engine was warm, so they took her into custody. She told them it's because she had just dropped me off at the Sheriff's Department, but they claim she did that to cover her tracks.

I can't stop recalling our lunch the other day when she was not only late, but dirty and disheveled. Why didn't I press her on that when I had the chance? Why didn't I insist she tell me the truth? Everyone involved in this case so far has lied to me, and I can't make sense of any of it. How can it be that everyone is lying about something? Is my ability to read people on the fritz? Can my gift be that far off? I don't trust myself to know these things anymore.

Why was I convinced I could persuade the Sheriff to see it my way? What was I thinking? I wish I had someone to talk to. I could call Zach, but he's not too happy with me right now. I know he doesn't believe Anne killed Barney, or tried to run down Gary, but now he's out $10,000 and in a terrible mood.

I have to be missing something; I just don't know what. If only I could bring on the visions with a snap of my fingers. That would be super helpful. I comb through Anne's iPad, that she left at my house, to study everything she put together. I vow to retrace my steps, leaving no stone unturned with our remaining suspects.

When I scroll through the list, I'm reminded that I still need to talk to Mrs. Robins at the country club to confirm Tyler's alibi. I'm not optimistic, but what else do I have to lose?

“Excuse me, is Mrs. Robins here by any chance?” I ask the clerk at the country club desk.

“She’s drinking coffee,” he points at a nearly empty lounge ahead. There’s two men at the bar and one woman sitting at a table, making it easy to guess which one must be her.

“Great! Thank you!” I’m finally getting somewhere. “Hi, excuse me, Mrs. Robins?”

“Yes?”

Jumbled thoughts race through my head. What am I supposed to say now? She’ll think I’m bonkers if I just blurt out a question like, “Where were you at 9 AM on Tuesday?”

“Uhhh...”

“Molly! I see you’ve found Mrs. Robins,” Tyler says when he approaches us. Mrs. Robins appears thoroughly confused. “You must be here to confirm my alibi,” he adds.

“Alibi?” she asks.

“Yes, if it’s not too much trouble, I need to ask where you were on Tuesday at 9:00 AM,” I tell her.

She looks up at Tyler in confusion, who nods.

“I was with Mr. Cross.”

I try not to let my disappointment show. She isn’t lying, and I can’t read Tyler.

“Why do you ask?”

“This will sound crazy, but I’m searching for answers as to who could have killed Barney Mullins. They told me Tyler had personal issues with him, so I just had to confirm where he was when Barney was killed.”

“He couldn’t have killed Barney; he was with me.”

"Thank you for your time. I'm sorry to have bothered you," I tell her. But as I turn to leave, a vision of a silver sedan comes through as clear as day. "Hang on a second, Tyler; what kind of car do you drive?"

"I have a silver BMW. Why?"

"Oh, I was just curious. It looks like there's a tow truck out front, and I didn't want you to lose your car."

"No worries. Mine is in the employee parking lot."

"Okay, good."

I'm glad he didn't double-check to see if I was telling the truth. Could Tyler have tried to kill Gary? Did he kill Barney? If he was giving Mrs. Robins a golf lesson on the back nine he couldn't have. Are the two events even related like the sheriff insists?

On the way home, I stop at the Calimaris Coffee Shop for a pick-me-up. I haven't slept much recently and need the caffeine to keep going. I stare wistfully at Stanley's Sign Shop across the street while I wait for my drink. How was it just a few days ago, I was there picking up my beautiful signs. I was so proud of myself. So excited to get on with my new career, and what's left of that?

Then I have a horrible thought. What if Jake and I have to move again? Because if I thought people were staring at me before, they at least tried to be subtle about it in the beginning. Now they just openly stare.

What will I do for work if I can't get my license back? I loved the idea of selling homes and helping people. Now I'm the town pariah.

While my mind runs wild with dark thoughts, it occurs to me that my sister could go to jail for a crime she didn't commit—a murder! And attempted murder. I plop down in the nearest seat, trying to calm my nerves. This is a disaster.

When my phone dings with a text, it's so loud I nearly jump out of the chair. Maybe I don't need the caffeine after all. My nerves are already threadbare.

A fisher just showed up at the sheriff's department. He was out on Lake Albus this morning and reeled in a golf club with Anne's name. Harvey texts me.

What does this mean? How could he catch a golf club like he would a fish? Just when I thought this couldn't get any weirder.

Get over to Lake Albus as soon as you can. The Sheriff's Department is sending a team of divers to search for the rest of the clubs.

I hurriedly pay for my coffee, run out the door, and hightail it to the lake. Did the real killer throw the clubs in the lake today? If so, that definitely rules out Gary. He's still in the hospital. But that also rules out Anne because she's in jail, so at least we have that.

When I arrive at Lake Albus, I'm dismayed to see the crowd of people gathered. They're everywhere. Reporters, sheriff's deputies, looky-loos; the whole town is here. Exciting stuff for this small village. It's not every day that the dive team is called to search for clues in a murder investigation.

I hurry over to Harvey when I finally spot him in the crowd. "This is good news, right? If someone threw the golf clubs in the lake this morning, it can't have been Anne."

"If they can determine that, yes. But if they decide they've been there for more than a day, then no."

Rats. I didn't think of that. I got so excited when he said someone found the golf clubs this morning, my mind leaped to them being dumped in the lake just recently. How can I be so lame? I keep jumping to conclusions that I shouldn't and disappointing myself. Now I think it would be better if the dive team can't find anything else.

The crowd cheers when a diver surfaces with a club. Then another diver comes up with the bag, making the crowd go wild. The killer must have dumped the clubs in the lake to cover his tracks. So much for locating him by finding the clubs in his house.

Sheriff Blake signals Harvey to come down to the dock.

"Wait here," he says sternly.

I don't want to make things worse, so I do as I'm told. After a brief discussion with the Sheriff, he returns looking grim. "The clubs are starting to rust. They couldn't have been thrown in the lake this morning."

Of course not. We can't seem to catch a break here.

"It gets worse," he adds.

"How is that possible?" I ask.

"The fisher told the Sheriff he comes here every day. He saw Anne on Tuesday around noon. He says it looked like she was throwing something in the water."

22

That's it. Anne is coming clean about where she was when Barney was killed. She'll tell me the truth if I have to drag it out of her. What if she and Barney fought, and she killed him in self-defense? I can't believe I'm even thinking this.

"Did you ask Anne where she was when Barney was killed?" I round on Harvey, sounding a little more confrontational than I'd like. Desperate times call for desperate measures.

"Absolutely not. I don't ask my clients that."

"Well, *I'm* going to ask her. Wait. The prison has visiting hours, right?"

"Of course, they do," he confirms.

After calling to ensure they'll let me see my sister, I head to the prison. It's at the far end of the village, so I have time to rehearse what I'll say to her. But after practicing several versions, I decide the best way is just to demand the answers outright. No need for nuance here.

My stomach flip-flops when I pull up to the heavily guarded prison compound. They house many types of criminals here, including some who could use their magic to escape. Those sections are guarded with ultra powerful spells. How did my sister ever end up in a place like this?

I pull up to the guard's booth, show my id, and give him my name. After confirming my identity, he waves me in, telling me which number spot I have to park in. The gravity of the situation hits me when I pull into my assigned section. My sister is in serious trouble and it's on me to get her out.

"From the look on your face I take it that you're not here with good news," Anne says after picking up the phone to talk to me through the thick, smudged plexiglass that separates us. She wears a gray prison jumpsuit that makes her look washed out and awful, but I won't tell her that.

"Why were you late to lunch the day Barney was killed?" I jump in without pretense.

When she rolls her eyes at me, I nearly lose it. This is serious, and she's acting like I'm nagging her about paying for overdue parking tickets.

"We've already discussed this. You know I'm always late. You came all the way here just to ask me that again?" her voice raises to a fevered pitch, betraying the fact she's pretending it was nothing.

"But you've never shown up with dirt on your face, twigs in your hair, and a broken shoe!"

"I told you I fell down when I was running to meet you."

"Stop lying to me!" I shout. When I strike my open hand against the glass, a muscled guard steps toward me. I'm upset and I've lost what little patience I had left. She could spend the rest of her life in prison for a crime she didn't commit, and she's still playing games with me.

Now the guards are on high alert because we're shouting at each other. It's only a matter of time before they kick me out for causing trouble, but I'm not leaving until I get the truth. They'll have to drag me out kicking and screaming. "They just fished your golf clubs out of Lake Albus!" I shriek.

"How did they get in there?" she asks, suddenly calm but genuinely perplexed.

For the first time since this started, she isn't lying. She really doesn't know how the golf clubs ended up in the lake.

"The angler who found the first club, and turned it into the sheriff says he saw you there the day Barney was killed and that you threw something in the lake. What were you doing there? What did you throw in the lake?"

"All right! Calm down. I threw my engagement ring in there," she admits reluctantly.

"Your engagement ring? Why didn't you just say that before? Why would you lie about...hang on, that was a $20,000 ring! You threw it in the lake? Are you out of your mind? Why didn't you just sell it instead?"

"See, that's exactly why I didn't want to tell anyone! I knew you'd judge me. It was a heat of the moment thing that I obviously regret now. My plan was to tell Barney I threw his expensive ring in the lake because I knew it would infuriate him."

And unlike the golf clubs, I doubt we'll find it now, so there goes our proof. I can't believe Anne threw a $20,000 piece of jewelry in the lake. $20,000! She could have paid for her own bail with it.

My mind churns the entire drive home. At least I know where Anne was for sure when Barney was murdered. I never really suspected her of murdering him, but I was starting to worry there had been a fight of some sort.

I stiffen when I spot someone waiting for me on the porch as I pull into the driveway. What now? Oh. Wait. Is that Tina from the office?

"Hi!" I wave to her while she flutters her wings in greeting. She's breathtaking.

While some pixies have the gift of magic, their real power lies in their ability to enchant unsuspecting creatures and humans. They're the ultimate seductress. Legend has it that if you allow yourself to fall under a pixie's spell, you're a goner!

"Tina! What a nice surprise!"

"Hello!" she giggles. Her laugh is so musical I swear I could listen to it all day. "I was just leaving you a note. I wondered how you were doing."

"I finally got my sister to admit where she was when Barney was murdered."

"I take it she was not with Barney?"

"She wasn't. Not," I hold up a finger, "that I ever really believed she killed him, but I knew she was lying about something."

"You look relieved."

"I am, but I'm still at a loss as to who killed him. Do you want to come in for a glass of iced tea while you're here?"

"I'd love that!" she says.

When Tina and I enter the house, Buster lazily lifts his enormous head, gives a soft bark, then returns to his nap. It takes all of a second for his head to pop back up, however, when he realizes there's a pixie in the house.

What in blazes?

Tina smiles as Buster's eyes widen. He slowly rises to his feet, untangling his long, gangly limbs as he does. His exaggerated air sniffs make us both laugh.

"He's never met a pixie?" she asks.

"Not that I know of. You should have seen his reaction the other night when Sheriff Blake showed up."

"Scary werewolf, huh?"

"Yep."

"Don't worry, boy; I don't turn into something frightful during a full moon. What you see is what you get." She holds her delicate hand out for examination while Buster tiptoes closer.

I don't know what this is, but it's so pretty. Smells good too. Zowie! It even tastes good!

Tina giggles when Buster takes a tentative lick of her hand. After that, he barks and jumps and twirls like a giddy toddler. I've never seen him that animated.

"You'll never get rid of him now," I warn her as she pets his head.

"Oh, that's okay. I love dogs."

And I love you!

Buster flops at her feet contentedly while I shake my head in disbelief.

"Most animals are naturally drawn to pixies," Tina explains.

"Do you get this reaction wherever you go?" I ask.

"Pretty much. And before you ask, no, it doesn't work on werewolves."

"Bummer!"

It's another gorgeous spring day in Melioras, so we take our drinks out on the porch. I add some fruit and cheese to a plate to snack on while Buster follows dutifully on our heels.

"So, what have you learned so far with your investigation?" she asks.

Just as I start to fill her in, my phone rings. It's Harvey! Oh, please don't be bad news; I cross my fingers. "I'm so sorry, but it's the lawyer. I have to answer this."

"No problem. Take your time."

"Hey, Harvey, I'd ask if you have good news, but you never do."

"They found a partial print on one of the golf clubs," he says.

"Just one? Do they know who it belongs to?" Please don't say Anne, please don't say Anne, please don't say Anne.

"Just one. They aren't sure if the rest were compromised by the lake water or if they were deliberately wiped down and they accidentally missed one, but--"

"Harvey!" I say so sharply that poor Buster jumps. "Whose fingerprint is it?"

"Collin Young"

23

"Collin killed Barney?"

"I didn't say that!" Harvey responds quickly.

I shake my head no, when Tina stares at me wide-eyed—false alarm.

"I just said his fingerprint was on one of the clubs," Harvey reminds me.

"But this is good news, isn't it? They'll bring him in for questioning!"

"Unfortunately, the Sheriff isn't interested. He said because the clubs were in the office that day, anyone could have touched them, so it isn't worth pursuing."

My shoulders sag. This is beyond frustrating.

"I'll keep working on it, though, okay?" he says.

"Okay, thanks," I tell him.

"Bad news?" Tina asks when I hang up.

"They found a partial fingerprint on the golf clubs that they fished out of the lake. It matches Collin Young."

"Are they going to arrest him?"

"No," I shake my head sadly. "Sheriff Blake says it isn't enough."

"Did you talk to Collin about Barney before?"

"He said he was visiting his pop pop in the nursing home when Barney was killed."

"You've verified this?"

"No, it seemed kind of weird to check up on someone's grandpa. Who would lie about something like that?"

"Plenty of people! Including a murderer."

"Good point."

"Did he say which nursing home?" Tina asks.

"I think he said, Shady Acres? Something like that?" I scratch my head.

"It must be Shady Pines."

"Yes! That's it!"

"Well, let's go." Tina leaps from her seat.

"Seriously?"

"This murder won't solve itself."

"All right, I'm willing to give anything a shot at this point. Sorry, Buster, back in the house."

Awww. Do I have to?

"That's the most pitiful face I've ever seen," Tina says.

"He's just playing us," I assure her.

If I stare at them long enough, they'll crack. Works every time.

"All right already. Stop looking at me like that. You can come."

Buster barks in response, running and leaping to the car like he just won the lottery.

Yes! Best day ever! Next, I'll talk her into stopping at the coffee shop drive through for some whipped cream.

Buster wedges himself into the back seat, purposely bumping his head against the sunroof until I open it for him to stick his head out. Whenever I do this, piles of people wave and take pictures. It must be quite a comical sight. Tina, of course, flits gracefully into the passenger seat. The difference between her delicate moves and Buster's blundering is significant.

I still feel a little creepy going to check on Collin's pop pop in the nursing home. But we can't afford to leave any alibi unchecked.

Shady Pines Nursing Home is nicer than I expected. The well-manicured lawn gives it a warm and inviting feel, while the early spring flowers seem to smile at us as I slowly drive along the half circle that makes up the entryway. There are several signs warning us it's for loading and unloading only, but I don't plan to be here long.

"Buster, if anyone tries to give us a ticket, you yell at them, okay?"

I'd like to see them try!

When Buster barks in agreement, Tina giggles and scratches his chin. If I didn't know better, I'd say he then winked at her.

"Hi, there," I tell the clerk at the front desk. "We're here to see Mr. Young."

"That's impossible," she says simply.

"Oh, I'm sorry. Are visiting hours over?"

"No, Mr. Young passed away six months ago."

"There must be some mistake. Mr. Young, he's Collin Young's..." I hesitate before saying it because it sounds so silly, "pop pop."

"Yes, I know who you mean. Again, he passed away six months ago. I'm sorry, were you a friend?"

"No, I never met him. Do you know if Collin has been here since his grandfather," I'm not saying the word pop pop again, "passed away?"

"I don't think so. Why would he?" she asks.

"No reason. Thank you for your time." That does it. In my book, anyone who's willing to lie about visiting their grandpa is probably a killer! "So, what now?" I ask Tina.

"We confront Collin. Get him to fess up."

"How will we do that?"

"I have my ways," Tina says.

"Collin, it is." During the trip to Collin's office, I fill Tina in on everything we know so far. But when we arrive, I realize I can't go in or risk getting arrested if the receptionist calls the Sheriff's Department again.

"Uhhhh, before we go anywhere, I have to tell you that I may have a slight problem," I hold up my fingers to show just how slight, even though I know it's bigger than that, "with the receptionist in Collin's office."

"Uh oh, what did you do?" Tina responds skeptically. If only she knew!

"Last time we were there, Sheriff Blake pretty much threatened to arrest us if we didn't leave. I really can't afford to get into any more trouble at this point."

"That's okay. I'm not afraid to go in. They don't know who I am."

"Okay, perfect-- wait! There he is!" I grab Tina's pixie arm, which is soothingly warm and soft. No wonder Buster has fallen under her spell.

When Collin gets into a white sedan, we turn to each other in surprise.

"White sedan," I whisper. "And look! It's a Nissan. The witness said she thought she saw the letter N. It totally fits!"

"Well, follow him!" Tina exclaims while Buster barks in agreement again. At this point, I think he'd agree to anything Tina says.

When Collin pulls out of the parking lot, we slip in behind his car. If he sees us in his rearview mirror, he'll wonder what kind of silliness is behind him.

I'm not convinced that it's the best idea for us to confront a murderer, but I'm hoping instead of going home, he visits a grocery store where we'll at least have witnesses.

But of course, that would be too easy, and because my luck has been horrendous lately, he heads for home. I realize it's now, or never, when he parks his car in his driveway.

"Let's do this," Tina says when he gets out of the car, opening the backdoor to collect his things from the back. At first, he sees only Tina and Buster, so he can't help but smile. When he recognizes me, however, the smile quickly fades.

"You followed me home, didn't you?" he snarls.

"We know why you lied to us about where you were when Barney was killed."

"You do?" he asks in confusion.

"You had to lie after you killed Barney. Once you threw the weapon in the bushes, you realized that the authorities would eventually look for the rest of the clubs, so you threw them in the lake. Then, somehow Gary Hill found out what you did and blackmailed you, so you tried to run him down with your car. Your white car!" I point out.

I gloat while preparing to phone the sheriff's office. Sure, Sheriff Blake might be annoyed at first, but once he realizes I figured out who really killed his cousin, I'm sure he'll change his tune.

The look of horror on Collin's face assures me he knows he's done. Although this obviously wasn't the safest thing to do - confront a killer face to face with no backup, but it's not like Sheriff Blake would have come with us. We didn't even need Tina's pixie magic to persuade him.

When Collin bursts into raucous laughter, however, I don't quite know what to do. He's so crazy he thinks this is funny.

"Why are you laughing?" Tina asks.

"I'm laughing because I can't believe the bizarre story you've cooked up."

"It's not bizarre! We just left the Shady Pines Nursing Home. You lied about your own pop pop!"

"I lied because I was at a job interview and didn't want anyone in the office to know. You confronted me in the middle of the lobby so what was I supposed to do? I'm already in enough trouble in that place as it is. If the people I was interviewing with call there, they might tell them I cheated on the CFA test."

Now it's my turn to laugh. Who invents a lame story like that? "Then how do you explain dumping the golf clubs in the lake to hide them?"

If he's surprised we know about the golf clubs he doesn't let on. "For the same reasons you just said...except," he holds up his hand when I open my mouth to interrupt him, "for the part where I killed Barney. After your sister threw her ridiculous tantrum by dumping those sweet golf clubs in the middle of the lobby, I waited until everyone else left, assuming, like always, they'd just expect someone else to clean up the mess.

I picked up the golf clubs, planning to keep them for myself. *That* was my way of getting back at Barney - not by murdering him! I brought them home to use them, but I haven't had much free time lately, so they've just been sitting in my garage. It wasn't until after Barney was killed that I realized the sand wedge was missing.

After you showed up to confront me about my past with Barney, I realized it was just a matter of time before someone came looking for the rest of the clubs. I knew I couldn't just walk into the police station and tell them that even though I took the golf clubs; I wasn't the murderer, so I threw them in the lake. As far as this Gary guy goes, I don't even know who that is."

"We'll need to confirm your newest alibi with the company you were supposedly interviewing with," Tina demands.

"Don't bother," I tell her dejectedly.

"Why?"

"He's telling the truth. He didn't kill Barney either."

24

Only moments before my alarm goes off the next morning, my cell phone shrieks instead, startling me out of a restless and disturbing sleep. Who is calling this early? I reach out to decline the call without thinking, but bolt upright when I realize it's Harvey.

"Harvey, what's going on? What happened? Is it Anne?" My sleep deprived mind leaps to when Jake asked his aunt if anyone had shanked her in prison.

"How soon can you get to my office?" he asks, his voice thick with urgency.

"I have to drop Jake off at school, but if this is an emergency, I'll get Zach to handle things. What's wrong with Anne? Was she shanked?"

"Was she shanked? No!" he exclaims. Is it just me, or is he trying not to laugh? This is where a person's mind goes when they live with a ten-year-old with an active imagination. "Anne is fine. I have something you need to see, but it has to be in person."

"Okay. I can be there at 8:30."

"Fantastic. See you then."

After dropping Jake off, I head to Harvey's office, wondering what on earth could be so urgent we have to meet in person.

"Hi Lena, I'm here to see Harvey," I tell his chain-smoking secretary, who has worked for him ever since I can remember. I'm amazed she's still around. Sure, when you're a little kid, the adults all seem old, but as I get older, I realize Lena really is ancient.

"Hey there, Molly, go right in; he's expecting you," she tells me in her signature raspy voice.

"Harvey, what's going on?"

"C'mere, pull up a seat." He gestures to the nearest chair. "Watch this," he says, pointing to the monitor after I pull up a chair beside his desk.

It's a video of Tyler, who, from his bloodshot eyes and slurred speech, is clearly drunk. He's holding a golf club, although I don't know what kind of club because, like my sister, I don't golf. The video was filmed while he leans against a silver BMW. What I can't tell is whether someone else is holding the camera or if he propped it against something.

"Hey *Barney*," he drawls in a sinister voice. "You're a big fat jerk; you know that? You knew I really liked Irene. And even though you were engaged to someone else, you just couldn't leave it alone. You couldn't stop until you lured her into your sick web of deception. You weren't even interested in her until I was. But oh no, you always have to win. I wish I had never even told you that I liked her. Well, watch your back, buddy, because I'm coming for you. When you least expect it." After he swings the golf club menacingly, he accidentally hits the camera, sending it flying. Then he curses, and the camera goes black. So much for being a peace-loving elf.

"Harvey, what kind of golf club is that?"

"It's a driver."

"Oh."

"You were hoping it was a sand wedge, weren't you?"

"Yeah, but still. He's holding a golf club while leaning against a silver car, threatening to kill Barney. Did you show Sheriff Blake yet?" My heart is sprinting, I'm so excited. This is it. This is our big break.

"As you well know," Harvey reminds me, shaking his head. "The Sheriff hasn't been helpful to our side, so I wanted to show you first so you could do your thing. Not that I'm encouraging your interference in the investigation or anything, of course, but if you were to conveniently come across Tyler and have a conversation with him before I could get this to the Sheriff, then, well, you know..." he trails off.

"The first time I talked to Tyler, he said he was giving Mrs. Robins a golf lesson on the back nine - specifically the 16th hole - when Barney was killed."

"Did Mrs. Robins confirm this?" Havey asks.

"She did. But after I talked to them, and just as I was leaving, I had a vision of a silver car. When I asked Tyler about it, he confirmed he drives a silver BMW. But I haven't been able to connect it to anything until now."

"I know you said his alibi checks out, but given this video evidence, I think you should talk to him again."

"He even told me that he and Barney had made up, and it was all good."

"Doesn't look like it's all good to me."

"I'll head to the country club right now and have another chat with our friend Tyler," I tell him.

When I arrive at the country club, there's a group of angry women gathered around the front desk firing demands at the clerk. Apparently, the washing machines aren't working properly, so there are no clean towels available. The clerk assures the women they're working on repairing the appliances as fast as they can, but until then, they'll have to do without.

I wait patiently for the group to clear out so I can ask the harried desk clerk about Tyler. While I wait, I scan the bulletin board to pass the time. There's nothing unusual on it - a coupon for $50 off a blowout in the hair salon, a lost and found notice regarding someone's locker key, a sign-up sheet for the upcoming Spring Spectacular Tournament - but my jaw drops when I see the notice that holes 16 through 18 are closed for an additional week due to sprinkler repairs and the club apologizes for the inconvenience. The dates listed show that the area was closed the day Barney was killed, and more importantly, when Tyler and Mrs. Robins claimed they were in the middle a golf lesson.

Tyler lied. Mrs. Robins lied. Did I just find my killer? What if Tyler killed Barney, then Gary found out about it and tried to blackmail him, not Collin? Right theory, wrong person.

I have to know where he is right now. I wedge myself through the ladies, who are still hassling the clerk.

"Excuse me! Excuse me!" I beg, pushing through the grumpy women.

"Please, wait in line!" the clerk urges me.

"This is an emergency!"

"What is it?" he sighs in exasperation.

"Just one question. Is Tyler here?"

"No," he rolls his eyes, because I'm sure the ladies ask that question all the time. "He's off today!"

"Thank you!" I tell him before squeezing back through the crowd, then sprinting for the front door. I'm so eager to find him I get in my car and take off before I realize I don't even know where to look. I'll have to go home where I can work without distractions to figure it out. I'll call Tina. She might know where I could get an answer.

I reach for the dashboard to call Harvey to let him know Tyler lied about his alibi, but he beats me to it by calling me first. "Hey Harvey, great timing. You won't believe what I just found out--"

He cuts me off. "--Anne is considering a plea bargain."

What the what? "Plea bargains are for guilty people. Or for people who squeal on their friends, aren't they? We know she didn't kill Barney; why on earth would she even discuss a plea bargain?" This is a joke, right? I'm being punked.

"The District Attorney offered her a deal. Plead guilty to involuntary manslaughter; she'll only serve a few years, then get released on good behavior. But if she doesn't take this deal, and she's convicted of murdering Barney and trying to murder Gary, she'll spend the rest of her life in jail."

"No! No! No! She can't do that. I won't let her! I'm *this* close to discovering who really killed Barney and who tried to kill Gary. I just know it. When I was at the country club just now, I found out that Tyler lied about where he was when Barney was killed. As soon as I can find him, I'll confront him. I'll take Tina with me, and she can use her pixie magic to force him to confess. I just need a little more time. Anne hasn't accepted the plea bargain yet, has she?"

"We're meeting with the DA later this morning to discuss specifics."

"Do not let her accept any kind of deal, Harvey. I'll go to the prison right now. I have to see her before she does something she'll regret for the rest of her life."

"Okay, I'll hold it off as long as I can," he says.

My trembling fingers push the red button on the dashboard screen to end the call. How could Anne even consider pleading guilty to something she didn't do? Sure, it looks bleak. Yes, every lead has been a bust so far, but the new evidence that points to Tyler is serious.

Why would he lie about his alibi and claim that he and Barney had made up if he wasn't guilty? Plus, he has a silver car. I thought Gary was blackmailing Collin, but he could have just as easily been blackmailing Tyler instead. As soon as I talk Anne out of this plea bargain nonsense, I'll track down Tyler, he'll confess, and everything will be right again.

I press harder on the gas pedal; I have to get to the prison before Anne does anything stupid. But when I see them out of the corner of my eye, I slam on the brakes, causing everyone behind me to slam on theirs as well. Screeching tires, honking horns, and angry shouts force Tyler and Irene, who are getting out of a silver car in front of Bartie's Bistro, to turn around and stare.

25

"Tyler! Tyler!" I shout, waving my arms like a mad woman after I spring from my SUV. The line of cars behind me grows longer while the drivers get angrier.

"Hey, uh, Molly?" Tyler calls back with a half-hearted, confused wave.

"Hang on a sec," I tell him when drivers yell things at me that I won't repeat in public. I deftly maneuver into a nearby parking spot while the drivers who were behind me speed past, shaking their heads and fists in disgust.

Sheez. You'd think they'd never confronted a murderer. Irene's eyes narrow into angry slits as I approach. Then, in a blink, she drops the angry look to hide behind Tyler.

"What the heck?" he mutters.

"Don't hurt me!" she exclaims.

"Who's hurting you?" Tyler asks.

He's at a complete loss about what's going on. Or at least he's pretending to be. That's okay; he'll know what's happening soon enough.

"Look out! Don't come any closer!" Irene cries, clutching the back of Tyler's arms like I'm heading for them with a golf club.

"Irene, what is wrong with you?" Tyler asks again.

"Your sister tried to run down my brother!" She waggles a finger at me.

"My sister did no such thing! Besides, it's not like he died. Unlike Barney!"

"He's in serious condition!" she exclaims defiantly. "Thank goodness that person stopped to help. Otherwise, I don't know what would have happened," she sniffles, wiping a fake tear from her otherwise dry eyes.

"It's okay," Tyler places a comforting arm around her.

Drivers slow down to stare at the unfolding drama. Oh sure, now they're interested in what's happening.

"I just need to talk to Tyler for a moment."

"Sure, what's up?" he asks.

"Remember when my sister and I asked you where you were when Barney was killed?"

"Oh, not that again!" Irene sneers, forgetting she's supposed to be afraid. "Your *sister* killed Barney. Tyler would never hurt anyone!" she shouts.

"I'm just here to clear up some confusion on my part," I offer.

"What do you need to know?" he asks.

"You said you were giving a golf lesson to Mrs. Robins on the back nine. Hole 16, to be exact."

"That's right."

Even though Tyler is an elf, and my attempts to read him so far have been unsuccessful, I try one more time.

Nothing.

"In addition, you told us that you and Barney had made up, but I just saw the video you made. The one where you threaten to kill him for stealing Irene from you."

"You threatened to kill Barney?" Irene asks in shock.

"I was drunk," Tyler explains. "I was just messing arou--"

Before he can finish any explanation, a shiny black Mercedes screeches to a halt in the middle of the street, right where I had been only moments before. This block has seen some action today.

"How dare you!" a red-faced, screaming Mrs. Robins, dressed in her finest tennis skirt, catapults from the car, stomping toward our group on the sidewalk.

Tyler's usual cheerfulness drains from his face, leaving Irene looking genuinely confused.

"How could you?" Mrs. Robins' voice pitches higher. With her fists clenched at her sides and her face contorting in anger, I realize I've never seen anyone that upset.

"You told me nothing was going on with her, yet here you are. And you," she rounds on me, still so rageful that I take a step back. "Is this why you wanted to know where Tyler was? Because you're messing around with him too?"

"What?" Irene snarls.

I take two more steps back, waving my hands in innocence. I'd laugh at the thought of Tyler and me if I weren't so scared. "No way! I'm clearly too old for--uh, never mind, no, I'm not involved with him. I barely know him."

Then it hits me. When I asked Mrs. Robins where she was when Barney was killed, she said she was with Tyler. My reading told me she wasn't lying. "*You* said you were giving her a golf lesson, but *you* said you were *with* him." I point at Mrs. Robins.

"That's right; we were enjoying our usual weekly morning meet-up at the hotel."

"Is she for real, Tyler?" Irene asks.

"Uhhh," is all he can come up with.

"Of course I'm for real. Where do you think he got that expensive car he's chauffeuring you in?" Mrs. Robins screeching is still so high pitched that birds in a nearby tree take flight.

Oops. That answers that question. As afraid as I am to even speak to this woman, I must confirm what they're telling me. "So, on the morning that Barney was killed, you swear Tyler was with you at the hotel."

"That's right, sweetie. Here's a tip. If you believe all the promises he made to you, you better re-think it. He's a liar and a cheat. And I want my car back," she demands, her hand thrust forward.

Tyler sheepishly digs in his pocket for the keys, slowly handing them over to her. When I wondered why Irene picked Barney over Tyler, I guess I shouldn't have. This girl has a type.

The thought that any of these men could have gotten the golf clubs through Irene flickers briefly in my head. But then it disappears just as quickly when my phone rings. I hate to tear my attention away from the Tyler mess, but it might be Harvey or even my sister.

"Hello?"

"Hi, is this Molly Fitzle?"

"Yes, it is." This better not be a sales call!

"Hello there, dear. It's Mrs. Kennets, across the street from the Baker house."

"Yes, hello, Mrs. Kennets. Can I call you right back? This isn't a great time." I'm worried she's calling to play me a song on the ukulele.

"No problem, dear. I was just calling because you said I should let you know if I saw anything happen at the house."

"Oh! Yes! You're right. What's up?"

"A young woman pulled up to the house, parked in the driveway, and then unlocked the door. I noticed she didn't use the lockbox, so she must have her own key. I've always thought that might be useful.

Better than hiding a key under the welcome mat. If I had one in a lockbox, I'm the only one who could access it. Do they sell those at the hardware store?"

"Mrs. Kennets, what is the woman doing now?" I sigh.

"Oh! Yes, it looks like she's inspecting the house."

"Thank you so much. I appreciate your letting me know."

Why is this woman inside my house? I mean my listing. Yes, I still consider it my listing even though I don't have a license, and I'm sure that after everything that's happened, even if I get my license back, I won't be selling that particular house anymore. Should I call Mr. Lange about this? Should I continue to watch the drama here? I still have to go to the prison!

Even though I can't read Tyler, I can sure read Mrs. Robins, and she's 100% telling the truth. The bad news is, Tyler couldn't have killed Barney if he was with her, and I'm rapidly running out of suspects to question.

Because the Baker house is just a couple of minutes away, I could swing by just to see who's there. I'm sure it won't take long. Then I'll go right to the prison. I swear.

26

When I park in front of the Baker house, I'm delighted to discover the crime scene tape is gone. My sign is still here but crooked now. I'd straighten it, but why bother?

There's a rental car parked in the driveway, and the front door is open with the lock box hanging from the knob untouched. Mrs. Kennets was right; whoever is in there has their own key. What is happening? Unease gnaws at me. I shouldn't just walk into the house when I don't know who's in there.

I should call Mr. Lange and then go to the prison to talk my sister out of this ridiculous idea of accepting a plea bargain. Yet something calls to me from inside the house. It's an uneasy energy that I just can't shake. Not the dark energy that I felt when we were about to discover Barney's body, but a nagging, anxiety ridden energy instead.

That settles it. I'll peek inside the house, make sure everything is all right; then I'll go to the prison. I swear. I'll just be a couple of minutes.

After I step out of my car, I can't miss Mrs. Kennets peering through the curtains at me. When I wave at her, the big glasses disappear.

"Hello? Anyone here?" I call out softly from the doorway. I jump when a woman suddenly pokes her head out of the kitchen.

"Can I help you?" she asks.

"Hi there, I'm Molly Fitzle. I'm the listing agent." I point to my yard sign. "Is everything all right here?"

"Yes, of course; hello, I'm Maureen Baker, Mr. Baker's niece."

"Oh! Phew. What a relief. After everything that happened, I was worried that you were someone who shouldn't be here."

"Let me guess. Mrs. Kennets called you."

"You know her too," I laugh.

"I just wish she'd seen someone over here when the murder happened," Maureen tells me.

"You and me both, girl. Although, technically, she saw someone. I just don't know for certain who it was."

If Maureen knows my sister is in jail for the murder, she doesn't let on. "Have you been in the" she points to the ceiling, "attic?" she whispers.

"I discovered the body, so yeah, I've been in the attic."

"Oh no! I wasn't thinking. I'm so sorry you had to go through that. Would it be rude of me to ask you to go up there with me? I totally understand if you don't want to. I'm a little nervous about going alone."

"Oh, I'm fine. I'll go with you." But I swear if there's another body, I quit. No need to give my license back. They could keep it, as far as I'm concerned.

"Mr. Lange told me that even though the biohazard cleaners mopped up the pool of blood, the old wooden floor is stained, and I should have it sanded. The company I talked to needs a picture."

"If you're ready, I'm ready," I tell her calmly.

"Let's do this," she says, squaring her shoulders, heading for the stairs. When we reach the top, she pauses, making my heart skip a beat. If she screams, I'm out of here.

"Are you okay?" I ask.

"This isn't as bad as I thought it would be," she sighs with relief.

Thank goodness. No body. "It was right there," I explain, pointing to the dark spot on the floor. Mr. Lange was right. While the blood is gone, there's a stain that needs sanding out.

"Were you scared when you saw it? The body, I mean? I would have been so scared."

"I was mostly in shock," I tell her.

"I guess Irene and her fiancé weren't interested in buying the place," she says so suddenly I'm sure I imagined it.

"Excuse me?" She didn't just say the name Irene. Surely, I misheard her.

"Irene told me she wanted to show the house to her fiancé because he might buy it for them. What is it?" she asks upon seeing the crazed look on my face.

"You aren't talking about Irene Hill are you?"

"Yes! That's her. Do you know her? She's a very distant cousin. Like a tenth cousin once removed or something. Technically, I'm not even sure that makes us related." She shrugs.

"What's her fiancé's name?" I ask.

"I don't think she told me. I gave her the lock box code and told her to help herself, but that was the last I heard about it, so I guess they weren't interested. She was actually supposed to meet me here today because she thought she misplaced something, but I haven't seen anything unusual, have you?"

"No, just the dead guy. I'm sorry, I have to take this," I tell her when my phone rings, interrupting my thought process about Irene once again.

"No problem," she waves her hand.

But when I pull my phone from my pocket, there's no call. "How embarrassing," I tell her. "It's your phone."

"Uh, no," she holds her phone up. "I didn't actually hear any ringing."

"Wow, that's really weird." I was sure I heard a phone. I must be losing it if I hear phantom ringing.

"Could you wait here a moment?" Maureen asks. "I left the contractor's number in the car, and I need to text him a picture of this," she explains, pointing to the floor.

"Sure, I can wait."

"Thank you so much; I'll just be a moment."

After she scurries out the door, I hear it again. It's a ringing phone. I double-check my phone just to be sure. Nope. Not my phone. Then I hear it again. I twirl around on my heel, trying to figure out where it's coming from.

"What the heck?" I whisper when I see what looks like a piece of narrow black metal wedged in a gap between the floorboard and the wall. This is definitely where the sound is coming from.

Kneeling down, I then stick my finger in the gap to pull on the metal, which slides out. Turns out it's not a piece of metal; it's a phone. It isn't ringing now either, but as I hold it in my hand, the anxiety ridden energy is so strong the phone practically vibrates with it.

When I tap the screen, I get a red bar telling me there's 1% battery strength left. How long has this been in here? Whose is it? When I tap the screen again, it asks for a passcode.

Rats. What's the passcode? When the numbers 1234 flash in my head, I immediately discount the vision. It can't be that easy, and I'm not exactly confident in my psychic abilities these days. Maureen is still in her car looking for the phone number, and I really want to see who this phone belongs to before she gets back.

"Here goes nothing," I whisper. 1234. That did it! It's open! A lengthy text message thread pops up. There's one from early Tuesday morning.

You left your watch at my house, and I want to make sure you get it back. Meet me at the Baker house on Rosemary Street at 8:45.

Holy smokes. This is Gary's phone!

27

Proof that Gary lured Barney here, then killed him! After I tap open the phone again, Maureen exclaims, "Found it!" so suddenly I nearly drop the phone. Right as the battery runs out and it goes dead. Of course, the battery dies right now. Cripes! I stuff it in my pocket before turning to face Maureen.

"Found it!" she says again, waving the card for me. "Hey, are you okay? You look like you've seen a ghost," she says before clapping her hand over her mouth in horror. "I shouldn't say stuff like that in here, should I?"

"This attic is getting a little creepy," I lie to her. It's not a total lie. The phone part is creepy, but not the attic.

"You're right. Let me take a couple of pictures, and we can be on our way."

"Sure, go ahead," I tell her. My brain is in overdrive. I'm finally holding proof in my hands that my sister didn't kill Barney. Or rather, in my pocket. This is absolutely, positively bonkers, that I have to wait until we get out of here to follow up.

By the time Maureen finishes and we get to our cars, I'm a nervous wreck. I have to see what's on this phone. Of course, it's a different brand than mine. I'll have to stop at the store for a charger.

How did it get wedged in the floorboards? Maybe Gary and Barney struggled, and he dropped it? Part of me knows I should go straight to the Sheriff's Department with it, but the other part reminds me that so far, the Sheriff has rejected every other piece of information I've provided. How would this be any different?

I need to take pictures of everything on the phone, then take it to the Sheriff. If he dismisses me again, maybe Harvey can do something. So far, everything has just been theory, but here's actual, physical proof that Gary lured Barney to the Baker house.

After the briefest stop at Target in the world's history, I race home with the new charger. Once I plug it in, it fires to life. Huzzah!

Never mind. Now it has to reboot. C'mon. C'mon. I tell it.

Finally! The main screen appears. I enter 1234 to access the text messages. This is it. Totally it.

Gary texted Barney telling him to meet him at the Baker house at 8:45 to get his watch. I already saw this one, but this must be who Mrs. Kennets saw outside the house. If she had agreed to look at a picture to begin with, I could have solved this a long time ago.

Hang on a second.

Are these messages from Gary or Irene?

When my phone rings again, I nearly fling it across the room I'm so frustrated. Why does it keep interrupting me?

"Hello?"

"Mom!"

"Jake, what's going on? Why are you calling from this number? It isn't your phone."

"I'm calling from the nurse's office at school."

"Why are you calling from the nurse's office?"

"I'm sick."

"What do you mean, you're sick? You were fine this morning." I swear I'm not a mean mom. He was perfect this morning. He's done this before when he had a test he didn't study for.

I stare longingly at Gary's phone. I really need to go through these messages.

"I have a stomachache. Can you come get me?"

"Are you sure you're not trying to get out of a test?"

"I'm sure. Please pick me up."

"Fine. I'll be right there."

I consider taking Gary's phone with me, but it's best to let it fully charge so I can document everything and then take it to the Sheriff. Jake might even know how to download the contents for me. Assuming he's not that sick.

"Hi, Molly Fitzle, here for Jake Fitzle," I tell the receptionist in the front office at Jake's school.

"Of course, Mrs. Fitzle." After searching for a while, she frowns. "Did you have a pre-scheduled appointment?"

"No, he just called from the nurse's office to tell me he's sick." I can appreciate the security, but this is a little ridiculous.

"It's not in the nurse's notes. Let me check to make sure."

"Okay." Am I a horrible mother for thinking he better not be making this up? I'm so eager to get home and go through the rest of the phone; this unexpected side trip is seriously stressing me out.

"Yes, Molly Fitzle is here to pick up Jake," the receptionist says into the phone. Then she pauses and sighs. "Jake Fitzle."

It's the real estate school all over again. What is wrong with these people?

"Okay, thanks."

"She'll be right up," she tells me.

Now I'm worried. What if it's serious? Like, life-threatening serious. He said his stomach hurt. What if his appendix burst? Should I call an ambulance? Why didn't they call one already? Then my mind jumps to the kids he said were picking on him. He told Anne the schoolyard was like a prison. He didn't get shived, did he?

I swear I'll never make fun of his overactive imagination ever again. Now I'm nearing the panic stage. I'm a horrible mother for doubting him.

"Mrs. Fitzle?" the nurse approaches me.

"Yes! Where's Jake? Should I call an ambulance?"

"There seems to be a mistake. Jake isn't in the nurse's office."

"Then where is he? How did you lose him already?"

"We didn't lose him. I assume he's still in class."

"He just called me from your office to tell me he was sick and needed to come home," I insist, my voice verging on hysterical.

"I've been in my office all afternoon and haven't had a single student."

A horrible feeling hits me so hard that I almost pass out. "Something is wrong!" I tell her.

"I agree. Kathy, I need a code yellow!" she barks at the receptionist. When they invented the new security system, they sent home a flyer with a list of codes. I don't remember most of them, but yellow is obviously some kind of alert. Kathy pushes a button on the console and special lights throughout the building flash yellow.

I just pray it doesn't turn red, which is the only one I remember for sure. Missing student.

“Which room is Jake Fitzle in right now?” the nurse asks.

“317,” the receptionist tells her. Her worried expression makes me nauseated.

“Let’s go!” the nurse exclaims, grabbing my arm and pulling me out the door.

28

The yellow warning lights reflect off the school's pristine walls with an eerie glow, while an ominous click click click noise from the lights rotating inside their plastic casing echos through the hallway. We start with a frantic walking pace, but switch to full-out running by the time we get to Room 317.

I am the worst mom ever. I've put getting my sister out of jail and getting my real estate license back over everything else, and where has it gotten me? I should have let Sheriff Blake handle this from the beginning. Even though he didn't seem that interested in thoroughly investigating the case, I'm sure he would have found the real killer eventually.

Now my child is in danger because of my neglect. I'll never forgive myself if something has happened to him. When we fly through the door of Room 317, Jake is genuinely shocked to see me.

"Mom!" he exclaims.

"Jake!" I cry, scooping him up in a massive bear hug. "You're all right!"

"Why wouldn't I be?" he asks, his words muffled against my shoulder. I refuse to let go, even when he squirms with embarrassment. "Mom, people are watching us," he whispers, while his classmates shift uncomfortably at the display of affection. They're just glad it isn't their mom in here squeezing the breath out of them.

"You called to tell me you were sick. Are you okay? You scared me to death," I repeat, checking every square inch of him for blood, bruises, or cuts.

"But I didn't call you. I've been in class the entire day. My phone is in my locker where it's supposed to be. You can even check it."

He isn't lying. Then it hits me.

Gary's phone...

My house...

The horrible sensation I experienced earlier wasn't about Jake. It was about the evidence I left at home. The way Gary entertained his customer with the Bert and Ernie impression flashes through my memory. He called me pretending to be Jake.

"Jake, call your father to take you home today." I turn to his teacher. "Don't let him leave with anyone other than Zach Fitzle," I tell her while she nods, making notes on the tablet in front of her. "I have to go."

I hug Jake again before rushing from the room.

Poor Jake. When this is all over, he'll probably have to switch schools again because his mother has humiliated him beyond repair.

I rush home to find the front door wide open, everything in disarray. In my mad dash to the kitchen, I pray it's still there, but I know it won't be. It's gone. The phone is gone. The charger is empty.

Dragging my hands through my hair in frustration, I could just about pull it out at this point. How could this happen? I realize I should look through the rest of the house to make sure Gary didn't steal anything else, but when I turn around, I scream bloody murder. There hangs Oliver. Frozen. In mid-air. Is he petrified? I've never seen such a thing.

Buster! My blood runs ice cold when I think of what he may have done to the dog. "Buster!" I scream. "Buster! Where are you?" First Gary pretends to be my kid, then he breaks into my house, stealing my only hope of freeing my sister, then he petrifies the poltergeist.

I swear if he's hurt our dog, he'll answer for it. Jake will be devastated if Buster is hurt – or worse. I sprint up the stairs three at a time, screaming Buster's name the entire way. And there he is. In my bedroom. Well, his back half anyway - sticking out from under the bed.

"Buster!" I scream for the hundredth time, my voice raspy from all the abuse. His tail slaps steadily against the floor while he attempts to crawl out from underneath the bed as gracefully as possible. Which is not very graceful at all when you're a 150-pound dog.

"Are you okay?" I fall to my knees, checking over every little bit of him like I did Jake. No blood or scratches. He seems fine.

You won't believe the afternoon I've had. I was sound asleep when these strangers broke into the house and started flinging our stuff around. I barked and barked at them, but they refused to leave, so I hid.

"I'm so glad you're okay!" I throw my arms around him like I did Jake, only Buster isn't embarrassed. After our joyful reunion, I head back downstairs with poor Buster who has attached himself to me. I scour the kitchen hoping somehow the phone just got knocked to the floor, and I missed it earlier, even though I know that isn't what happened.

I'm disgusted he broke into our home and rifled through our things. The place where we're supposed to feel safe and secure. A place where we invite friends and family to enjoy special occasions with us. Now Gary has tainted that, and it will never be the same.

"Oliver, what are we going to do with you?" It must be a spell. I know that Gary is a demon, but I didn't know he could perform magic. And why did he need to petrify him? Thank goodness Buster hid from them. I bet Zach can break the spell. I hope whatever it is; it isn't painful. He's a poltergeist, after all. Does he even feel pain?

I know I threatened to call the medium to get rid of him, but now I feel bad. I don't need a frozen poltergeist floating in my kitchen though. Not the decorating scheme I was aiming for.

Now he can't even confirm that it was Gary. If he could talk, he might be useful in trying to persuade the Sheriff. Especially now that the evidence is missing.

I wonder if I could move him into the corner? I'm almost afraid to touch him, though. Not knowing what kind of spell was used to freeze him like this, I'd hate to get frozen myself. Nope. I'll just leave him as is and let Zach deal with it.

If I thought finding Barney's body during a showing was the worst day ever, I was sorely mistaken.

"Oh, what now," I groan out loud when my phone dings with a text.

It's Harvey.

Your sister just accepted the DA's offer. She signed the plea bargain agreement.

29

It's hard to estimate how long I've been sitting at the kitchen table with a large glass of wine when Jake walks in the front door, Zach right behind him. Buster, who hasn't left my side since I found him in the bedroom, scampers through the kitchen to greet them.

"Hi, boy!" Jake says.

You'll never believe what happened to me today. I was so scared!

"Molly! Molly!" Zach calls out.

"I'm in the kitchen."

"What happened to the living room?" he asks. "Whoa!" he exclaims, stopping in his tracks when he sees me with wine in the middle of the afternoon. "Whoa!" he repeats himself when he sees Oliver floating frozen above us. "Why can't I stop saying whoa?" he asks, his hand on his chest. "What happened?"

"Hey, Mom, why is the living room -- whoa!" Jake shouts when he sees Oliver.

Zach puts his arm across Jake to prevent him from moving any closer.

"Why is Oliver frozen?" he asks.

"It's a looooong story," I groan, hanging my head.

"Are you drunk?" Zach asks.

"No. But I wish!"

"What's going on, Molly? Should I be worried?"

"My sister just pleaded guilty to murdering Barney, and Gary Hill broke in here to steal the only evidence I had to clear her."

"But your sister didn't kill Barney. Even I know that."

"Tell me something I don't know," I mutter into my glass. "Hey, can you figure out what's wrong with Oliver? Can you thaw him out or whatever? Or is he a goner? Again."

"The magic is dark," he says, scrunching up his forehead like always when he's working on a problem. "But it isn't sophisticated."

He ponders Oliver's predicament while Jake and I continue staring at him. He's just floating up there, slowly rotating like there's a breeze pushing him in a circle. It's mesmerizing, really.

"This requires a wand," Zach decides, pulling his from his back pocket.

Wizards like Jake and Zach don't need wands for simple magic, but for the more challenging spells and especially for the dark spells, their wands give them additional power. Zach slowly traces a glowing circle around Oliver, then steps back to consider it.

"It's a petrifying spell, but not a particularly strong one. If he isn't back to his usual obnoxious self by tomorrow, let me know. There are a few counterspells I can try."

"Okay."

"Wait, I thought Gary was in the hospital," Zach points out.

"He was. But after I got home and saw that someone had broken into the house, I called them. They said he left two hours ago *and* against medical advice."

"That still doesn't prove he was in the house."

"Who else would be that desperate to get the phone?"

"Are you sure you don't want to call the Sheriff?" Zach asks. "Besides, I'm sure once Gary he got the phone, he destroyed it."

I shake my head sorrowfully. "What good would it do to call the Sheriff? My sister has already pleaded guilty to murdering Barney and trying to kill Gary. If he wasn't interested in investigating anyone else before, he really wouldn't be now."

"That's it then. You're both coming to stay with me for a while," he insists. "Of course, you're coming too, Buster," he adds to Buster's booming bark.

I'm never letting you people out of my sight again!

The weather the following day perfectly complements my mood. Heavy storm clouds gather overhead while fat raindrops splash against the window at Zach's house. I've planted myself in front of the giant picture window, arms crossed in defiance, while I scowl at the world.

When the neighbor across the street pulls up to their house in a gray car, I turn to Jake. "Hey, you know your cars. Is there one with an N in the logo?"

"Nissan?"

"Besides that one."

"Some people think this looks like an N," he offers, showing me logos on his laptop.

"That's a K."

"I know, but if you squint your eyes a little..."

"Yeah, I can see it now. I'm sure it's all for naught, but I really wish we could find that car and, more importantly, who was driving it."

"Who's that?" Jake points outside.

At first, it's hard to tell with the rain, but when she draws closer, I realize it's Tina. How did she know I was here?

"Hurry up! You'll get soaked!" I caution as she makes her way to the front door. "How did you know where to find me?"

"I have my ways," she smiles warmly. "Buster!" she exclaims when he prances out of the kitchen after realizing his favorite pixie is here. I'm sure he thinks she came just for him.

"Gosh, you're pretty," Jake stares at her.

"You must be Jake," she says.

He nods his head wordlessly.

"Hey Molly, why is Buster so-- oh my goodness," Zach breathes.

"And you must be Zach."

Zach also nods wordlessly while Jake hasn't stopped nodding. Buster wags his tail so hard I swear it could fall off. Ah, to be a pixie.

"I thought I'd drop by to see how you're doing and ask you if you wanted to go somewhere. Shopping? Lunch? A movie?" she asks.

"Could we go to my house real quick?"

"Sure. Did you forget something?"

"No, but Zach thought that Oliver could be back to normal by now, so on the off chance he can tell me something helpful, I think we should try."

"We'll be back in a while," I tell the three boys, who seem to have lost their voices. I just shake my head while Tina giggles.

"Thanks for coming to get me," I tell her once we reach my car.

"I figured you could use a break."

I fill her in on everything that has happened since I last saw her. But the closer we get to my house, the more nervous I get. What if Gary came back? What if I can't bear seeing the mess he made of my things? When I left yesterday, I was in shock. But what will it be like today?

"We don't have to do this," Tina offers, sensing my hesitation.

"I'll be okay. I want to make sure the house is still in one piece."

"I'm sure Gary is long gone," she says.

"That's a good thing *and* a bad thing."

I cautiously enter the house, half expecting something to jump out at me. I'm grateful that it's exactly as I left it. Or should I say, as Gary left it, considering the living room is still a mess. No Oliver, though. I never thought I'd say this, but I'll be disappointed if we can't de-petrify him.

"This is awful," Tina says sympathetically. "If you want, I can help you clean up."

"Eh, let's look for Oliver first."

We find him still floating in the kitchen, but partially thawed. He can't talk yet, but at least he's moving more than he could yesterday.

"Oliver, can you move your head?" I ask.

He affirms by nodding.

"Are you in pain?"

This time he shakes his head again. That's good.

"Do you know who did this to you?"

He nods enthusiastically.

"Was it Gary Hill?"

Another quick nod.

"See there! You knew it!" Tina says, clapping her delicate hands.

"Yeah, but I'm really not surprised."

"Wait, what's he doing with his fingers?" she points out.

"He's just wiggling them, I think, probably checking to see they're all there."

Oliver shakes his head.

"He's trying to tell us something!" Tina exclaims, at which Oliver nods enthusiastically. "He's holding up two fingers!" she points out. Oliver nods again.

"You're right!" I agree.

"He's either flashing a peace symbol at us or showing us the number two."

"Knowing him, it's not a peace symbol," I tell her.

When Oliver nods again, I ask, "Are you saying two?"

Another nod. This could take all day.

"Two people?" Tina asks, shrugging at me.

This time Oliver nods so hard he almost tips over.

"Gary *and* Irene?" I suggest, surprising even myself when the idea pops into my head.

This time Oliver nods so hard he tilts to the left, hitting his head on the wall. That was a weird noise coming from a ghost.

30

"You know where we need to go next?" I ask Tina.

"The Sheriff's Department?"

"The Swift Auction House in Tenebris Village."

"Why would we go to an auction house?"

"The first time Anne and I talked to Gary, he told us he was in Tenebris--"

"--which is an hour away." Tina points out.

"Yes. He told us he was there picking up some expensive scotch that his boss won in an auction."

"I'm confused."

"At the same time Barney was killed." I clarify.

"Ah." She nods.

"But later, Anne and I overheard his boss yelling at him for not picking up the scotch he won in the auction."

Tina's jaw drops. "What did Gary say when you confronted him about the lie?"

"We never got the chance. Gary was in the accident right after that."

"How fortuitous," Tina says.

"It sure looks like it, doesn't it?"

"Why don't we just call them?"

"I tried. They refused to tell me anything over the phone. But I'm thinking if I had you with me..."

"Tenebris it is! But can we stop for coffee first?"

"Are you sure you're not hoping for a cup of whipped cream like Buster?"

"No, I actually want coffee," she laughs.

I hope I'm not just trying to distract myself here by grasping at straws. I'm still not entirely sure what I'm looking for at this point. What I really need is that phone, but since it's gone, I have to try to put the other pieces of the puzzle together. There's something I'm missing, but I don't know what. It's nagging at me from the edges of my brain but it's unclear and frustrating.

"Hi there," I tell a man in the auction office who can't stop staring at Tina. "Could you tell me who's in charge of making sure the winning auction items are retrieved?"

"Uhh, yeah, that would be, uhh, Billy, the manager," he says, never taking his eyes off Tina.

"Could we speak to him?"

"Uhh, sure."

When Billy appears, it's obvious he isn't happy about being interrupted. Good thing Tina is with me.

"Hello, I'm Molly Fitzle, and this is Tina Lucas. We're from Melioras Village. I want to ask you about a bottle of scotch that the owner of the Partying Pony Bar won recently."

"We don't give out that kind of information."

"Please?" Tina begs, fluttering her wings.

"Which auction do you want to know about again?"

"It's for the owner of the Partying Pony Bar in Melioras."

"Oh, yeah, I remember that!" he exclaims, suddenly enthusiastic about telling us the story. "It was the weirdest thing. Dude was supposed to pick up his boss's $600 bottle of scotch. We prefer that the winners retrieve their winnings as soon as possible because if something happens to it, we're responsible.

"So, he makes an appointment to pick it up. Great. Then he calls to tell me he's delayed by family business and will be here late. Okay, fine. But a little while later, he calls *again* to tell me he can't come because it's turned into a family emergency.

"I had to reschedule several appointments that morning because of him, and then he never picked it up, anyway. What a hassle! His boss has won auctions before, and he's always reliable about picking them up right away, so this one was just weird."

We already knew Gary lied about where he was when Barney was killed, but this excuse about a family emergency almost makes the murder seem unplanned. It doesn't fit the idea of him luring Barney to the Baker house so he could kill him.

"So, he's been here before?"

"Sure. Lots of times."

"Weird question. Do you know what kind of car he drives?"

"How would I know that?"

"We were just wondering."

"You ladies sure have some weird questions. Is there anything else I can help you with?"

"No, I think we're good here."

"Come back anytime, ladies. Any time!" he says, staring starstruck at Tina.

"I swear it's two steps forward, one step back," I tell her as we walk back to the car. "I keep getting bits and pieces of information that point to Gary, yet not enough to put the whole picture together."

"Where to next?" she asks.

"I'm not sure," I moan. "I'm at a loss."

Just as we start to pull out of the parking lot, a man pounds on the passenger window, making us both scream. I roll down Tina's window, my heart racing from the unexpected interruption. What is this strange man doing? Should I even open the window?

"Billy said you were asking about Gary Hill's car?"

"Yes! Do you know what kind of car he drives?"

"I'm pretty sure he drives a gray Kia with dark-tinted windows. My mom has one just like it."

"Shoot, so no N," Tina says.

"Hang on a second." I search on my phone for the logo Jake showed me earlier. "Don't you think you could mistake that for an N? Especially if you were panicking after seeing someone nearly get run over."

"Yes, and the tinted windows could be why the witness didn't see who was driving," Tina exclaims. "Is it just me, or is this all really weird? Gary just happens to drive the same kind of car that we think nearly ran him over. That's a huge coincidence."

"Hang on a second. I have another idea," I tell Tina. I frantically search the internet for the phone number for Barney's office. "Please let me be wrong," I whisper while it rings. "Hello!" I tell the receptionist when she answers. "I'm calling for Irene Hill."

"Ms. Hill quit yesterday without notice. Is there someone else I can put you in touch with?"

"Do you know where I can find her?"

"No clue," she responds testily.

"Okay, thanks," I tell her, but she's already hung up.

I inhale deeply. Am I really about to say this out loud? "Irene killed Barney," I announce. "And now they're missing."

"Are you kidding me?" Tina exclaims.

"What if the reason Gary called the auction house to cancel is not that he had just killed Barney but because Irene did? It wasn't Gary's phone I found in the attic; it belonged to Irene instead. Gary didn't petrify Oliver. He doesn't have the ability. But Irene does."

"So, Irene killed Barney but later tried to run over her brother with his own car?" Tina asks.

"I didn't say I had all the details worked out yet, but I've been dismissing Irene all along because Mrs. Kennets said she saw Barney with a man. But the common denominator in this is Irene, not Gary."

"But how do you prove it without the phone?"

"I don't know," I shake my head.

"They must have destroyed it by now," Tina points out.

I maneuver the car onto the road while we drive silently for some time, mulling over everything that's happened so far.

"You know, Maureen told me she's remotely related to Gary and Irene," I point out. "Tenth cousins or something."

"Okay."

"This is a total longshot, but I remember from my real estate classes that when someone dies, they have to research property records for any additional property that heirs might be able to claim. What if the house on Rosemary Street wasn't Mr. Baker's only house? What if Mr. Baker owns another house where Gary and Irene could be hiding?"

"We're 20 minutes from the office. We could stop there to research the property records." Tina exclaims growing more excited by the moment.

"Let's do it!" I tell her.

That 20 minute drive seems to take forever, so by the time we finally arrive, we practically fly out of the car, we're so eager. We walk briskly toward Tina's cubicle when Myers falls in behind us.

"What are you doing here? You lost your license," he says.

"Temporarily suspended. Not lost," I tell him confidently while Tina nods in enthusiastic agreement. This is not the day for someone like him to take me down.

He then blathers on about how there really isn't a difference, and it's just a matter of time before they take it away, but I ignore him. After everything I've been through this week, I no longer care what he thinks. He doesn't get to decide how I feel about myself.

After grabbing the chair from my cubicle, I pause. My lonely real estate license is still propped up against the side of the desk. I'm surprised Myers didn't take it to the document shredding room. "I'll get you back," I whisper to it.

Tina logs onto the property records portal and searches under Baker.

"There's the house on Rosemary Street," I point out the entry.

"And will you look at that? Mr. Baker has a cabin in Steinley Forest," Tina announces, grinning ear to ear.

"Yes!" I exclaim, high fiving her.

"I knew you'd make a great agent," she insists.

"Let's go!" I tell her excitedly.

"You know that's two hours away, right?"

"Too far?" I ask.

"No, I just wanted to make sure *you* realized how far it is."

"I'm good if you're good," I tell her. "I need that phone."

"But I still think they destroyed it the moment they got the chance. What will you do when you find them?"

"Tina!" Mr. Lange shouts from across the room. "The neighbor from the Merrill Avenue house just called. A pipe burst in the house and there's water pouring everywhere."

"Oh no. I have to go," she cries.

"That's okay. I'll be fine."

"Are you sure?"

"Go. Deal with the flooding."

"Do not go there alone!" she scolds. "Take Zach. Or better yet, call Sheriff Blake. He's sure to understand."

I nod my head. I don't want to lie, but there's no way Sheriff Blake will listen to anything I say at this point. And Zach will just tell me to call the Sheriff too. I don't even know if Gary and Irene are there. It's senseless to get everyone else involved when it may be nothing.

As tenth cousins or whatever they are, they might not even know about the cabin. I could drive for two hours only to come up with nothing. When I get there, if Gary and Irene really are hiding out, then I'll wait for the authorities.

I get it. The smartest move would have been for them to destroy the phone, but I feel like Irene may have kept it. Just because. I know. I'm out of my mind. But what else do I have to lose?

I text Zach. "I have something important to do. I'll be gone all afternoon."

"But Jake says it's lunchtime."

"So get him some lunch!"

Like Zach doesn't know how to prepare lunch for Jake, or order a pizza. Jake certainly knows how to make a sandwich. They won't starve if I'm gone for a few hours. Actually, it will be a good lesson for them.

The trip to Steinley Forest is now or never.

31

While I'm entering the cabin's address into the GPS system, I remind myself this may be the most ridiculous thing I've ever done. Am I seriously about to drive two hours to a remote cabin in the woods on the off chance that a pair of killers are hiding there? Yes, I am.

I spend the first hour of the drive arguing with myself about what a lame idea this is. But what other option is there? The Sheriff won't believe me. *I* barely believe me. It's the only thing standing between my sister's freedom and years in jail. Even when she gets out, she'll still be a convicted felon.

Meanwhile, I lose my sister and my real estate license. I know I have to do this. I have to take this chance. I realize they may have been to the cabin and left already. There's a good chance they don't even know it exists.

Or, worst-case scenario, they're there, but I'm wrong about Irene wanting to keep the phone and she destroyed it. But if my instinct is correct and they *are* there and Irene still has the phone, then Anne is free. I still say I'm doing the right thing. It's my only hope.

After getting lost twice, yes, even with GPS help, I finally arrive at the turnoff road for Mr. Baker's cabin. The road is unpaved and full of twists and turns. I wouldn't want to drive it in the winter, although I imagine it's beautiful coated in sparkling white snow. Evergreen trees reach tall into the blue sky. A bold squirrel dashes across the road in search of an acorn, forcing me to slam on the brakes.

I'm surprised they even have addresses here. It would be just as easy to say it's that house that sits on the right after the 14th turn just before the rock formation that looks like a rocket ship. When the GPS tells me the cabin is about 300 yards to my right, I pull off the dirt road to hide my SUV under an unusually stout evergreen tree.

Now that I'm finally here, I'm convinced I'm absolutely, certifiably insane for doing this. Alone! Sadly, there are no signs of activity. No tire tracks. No footprints. Nothing. Gary and Irene can't be here. No one is here. I drove all this way for nothing.

But I need to walk around for a bit before returning home. My back is stiff after driving for two hours and I could use some lunch. Although I'm pretty sure I won't find that here. Not unless the squirrel is willing to share his acorns.

I trudge up the road in the direction I thought the cabin was supposed to be. The air smells of pine and wood. I breathe deep and soak up the silence. No traffic noises. No blaring horns. No blasting car stereos. Nothing. Just nature.

I continue ahead, stopping in shock when I spot smoke unfurling from a chimney. My heart skips a beat. Am I hallucinating? No! Someone is in that cabin. Then I see it. Gary's gray sedan. I throw my hand over my mouth to keep from whooping out loud. They *are* here!

I move closer to the treeline to stay out of sight. Ever so slowly, ever so quietly, I tiptoe toward Gary's car, ducking down behind it when I finally reach it. When I place my hand on the bumper to steady myself, a vision nearly knocks me onto my rear.

This is the car that almost ran into me the morning I was driving to the real estate school. The gray car with heavily tinted windows! I forgot all about it once I got my license. It must have been Gary fleeing from the house after Irene killed Barney.

What would have happened if he ran into me rather than narrowly avoiding me? Of course, I could have been injured, but what if the accident proved it was Irene who killed Barney? Could we have avoided the trauma we've been through this week?

Would my sister be at work right now instead of in jail confessing to a crime she didn't commit? Would I be showing homes to clients at the moment? I certainly wouldn't be sneaking around at a remote cabin in the woods.

I'm so busy pondering all this that I fail to hear the footsteps behind me.

"What do you think you're doing?" Irene says as I whirl around to find her pointing her wand at me with a furious expression.

Fiddlesticks!

"Stand up," she says.

I stand up slowly, worried if I startle her, I'll end up like Barney.

"Go!" she grunts, motioning to the cabin.

I calculate whether I can rush her successfully. Maybe without the wand, but it's too much of a risk with it. Given the look on her face, there's no telling what she'd do. If only I were a witch, I could defend myself. But until I can think of something better, I'll have to do as she says.

Dried pine needles crunch under our feet while we approach the cabin. The sound stands out painfully amidst the silence I was enjoying just a moment ago. Every so often, she jabs me in the back with her wand, delivering a painful shock.

"You don't have to keep doing that. I'm cooperating, you know."

"I know. I just like watching you jump."

“What the?” Gary says after I push open the door, and we step up into the cabin.

“Look who I found sneaking around outside,” Irene announces.

“Why were *you* outside?” Gary asks Irene.

“That’s your question? I find *her* lurking, and you want to know why *I* was out there?”

“Whatever. Did you see anyone else? She must have brought back-up.”

“I didn’t see anyone else,” Irene says.

Nope. I didn’t bring backup. I’m an idiot.

“You’re here for the phone, aren’t you?” Gary laughs. “It’s too late,” he sneers, sticking his face only inches from mine. “Irene destroyed it.”

32

"Yeah, I destroyed it," Irene cackles. "But even without the phone, we can't let her go. She'll run back to Melioras to tell everyone."

"I already told a ton of people I was coming up here." I nod. "When I don't return, they'll know something happened. They're probably on their way right now. They could be sneaking up to the cabin as I speak."

When Irene runs to the window, Gary laughs. "You moron. No one is on their way. She came here alone because they don't believe her. It's why she took the phone to her house instead of going straight to the Sheriff's Department. No matter what she and her sister told Sheriff Blake, he was convinced that Anne murdered his precious cousin out of jealousy. Your bizarre idea to take the heat off by nearly running me over paid off sis. Even if you did almost kill me in the process."

He laughs at my shocked reaction. "I knew I heard something in the alley after you two left the bar the second time, and my boss yelled at me for not driving to Tenebris Village to get his precious scotch. I also knew that meant you were closing in on us, and we had to do something drastic to distract everyone. It was supposed to end with a near miss, though. Not with me in the hospital. We got even luckier than we hoped when the Sheriff used it as an excuse to re-arrest your sister just because she has a silver car." Gary continues to laugh in a shrill, ugly way.

"As much as I love this trip down memory lane, we have to decide what to do next," Irene points out.

"Let's tie her up for now so she can't pull any tricks. We'll decide what to do with her body later," Gary insists.

"Why don't you let me go?" I beg. "It will take at least two hours to get back to Melioras Village. That gives you a huge head start. Like you said, Sheriff Blake is on your side, anyway, so you probably don't even need a head start. The phone is gone, so there's no proof, right? It will be my word against yours and no one believes me, anyway."

"It won't work," Gary responds, shaking his head. "We need way more than a few hours."

"I agree," Irene says. "Let's just kill her right now and be done with it," she says, raising her wand, and pointing it at my face while I try not to cower. I refuse to give her the satisfaction.

"No!" Gary shouts, shoving her arm down so forcefully that for a second I think she's going to turn the wand on him. "We've not having a repeat of Barney here. I don't need you killing someone else while I have to invent a grand cover up scheme. We're planning this one beforehand," he insists while tying me to a chair.

"How does it feel to come all this way for nothing?" he asks.

I consider telling him what I really think of him when I hear it. A phone. It's ringing. And it's not mine. I left mine in the SUV. Neither Gary nor Irene seem to hear any ringing. I can't help it, though, when my head whips to the side where I hear it.

"What? What are you looking at? Did you hear something?" Gary peers out the window.

"I knew she brought her friends!" Irene fires back.

"I told you. They don't believe her. Besides, I don't see anything," Gary responds.

"Then why did she turn to the window so suddenly? Like she heard something?" Irene points out.

"How am I supposed to know?" Gary snaps.

As long as I can keep them distracted and arguing with each other, there's still a chance I can figure a way out of this mess.

"Would you like to know how I found the phone in the first place?" I ask them out of the blue.

"More importantly, why should we care? Irene said she dropped it in the house while fighting with Barney. I assume you saw it while you were talking to Maureen. Yeah, that's right," Gary says when I look surprised. "Irene was supposed to meet Maureen to get the phone back. But then you showed up and screwed everything up."

Just keep going, I tell myself. You've got them on the defensive. "It fell into a gap in the floor," I explain.

"So?" Irene says.

When the phone rings again, I don't flinch this time. Not even a little. I was right. Neither Gary nor Irene hears it.

"You said Irene fought with Barney?" I stare at Gary while Irene squirms.

"You might as well tell her. She isn't leaving here anyway," he points out.

"Barney was livid. Even though I insisted he left the watch at my place, he knew I had stolen it from his house. When he saw me with the golf club as well, he really lost it. We struggled with the club before I wrenched it from his hands. Then I swung it at him. I expected him to duck, but he didn't. I didn't mean to kill him."

"Your phone must have slid across the floor and slipped into the gap. It was a perfect hiding spot. A normal person would never see it.

The cops didn't, and they went over the entire attic with a fine-tooth comb."

"So? It's gone, anyway. What does any of that matter now?" Irene asks.

"I heard it."

"What do you mean you heard it?" she says.

"Obviously, someone called you, and it rang. Duh!" Gary responds.

"Nope." This would be comical if it weren't terrifying.

"I know! It was a phantom ring!" Gary says, raising his hands and marching around like he thinks he's a ghost. "Everybody hears those at some point."

"I heard it psychicly."

"Ohhhh a psychic ring," Irene guffaws. "Got any winning lottery numbers you'd like to share? It's not like you'll be needing them."

"You're an idiot," Gary says suddenly while the grin slides from Irene's face.

"What?" she asks, confused.

"You said you destroyed the phone."

"I did." She shifts uncomfortably.

He points an accusing finger at me. "*She* just heard it ring. Didn't you?"

"I don't know what you're talking about."

When Irene pales, I knew I was right all along. It takes every bit of self-discipline I have not to shout, HA!

"I knew it! I knew I should have destroyed that phone myself. I knew there was a reason you insisted on taking care of it," Gary bellows. "You had to keep the phone to keep your texts and voicemails from Barney. That's why you were wandering outside just now. You were checking on the phone. Where is it?"

It's all I can do to keep from grinning from ear to ear. I'd also like to give a big fat "I told you so!" to anyone who doubted me. I know, I know, I have more important things to worry about - like staying alive. But still. It's nice to know I was right. Even though it seemed ridiculous.

"I'm not telling you." Irene pouts.

"Then *you* tell me!" he demands.

"Why would I tell you if you're just going to kill me, anyway?"

"Because I know where you live, remember? We can still kill you, then find your kid. And that sissy dog of yours, and--"

"Okay, okay, I'll show you where the phone is."

"Oh, no, I'm not falling for that. You'll try to get away."

"She's the only one who knows exactly where it is." I nod at Irene. "Even though I hear it ringing, I can't tell you where it is unless I follow the sound."

Irene glares at us. Her arms crossed in defiance. She's not giving up the location of that phone.

After some consideration, Gary unties me, then pulls me to standing while Irene brandishes her wand. "Let's g--"

Before Gary can finish the word go, Sheriff Blake blasts through the flimsy front door, sending pieces flying across the room, forcing us all to dodge them. Even more shocking though are Zach and Buster, who race in behind him. How did any of them get talked into this?

33

Irene fires a stream of blindingly bright orange sparks at them. But the Sheriff ducks, causing the spell to hit Buster instead, who yelps like someone stepped on his foot.

"Buster!" I cry out before he flees.

Chaos ensues, with Irene and Zach flinging dueling spells at one another. Sheriff Blake and Gary wrestle to the ground. Gary must be stronger than I realize when he holds his own with the Sheriff.

Meanwhile, I just stand there staring while the battle unfolds. I can't decide where to go. Forward? Backward? Left? Right? There's smoke and sparks and name-calling flying this way and that, while I'm rooted to the spot. I have to make sure Buster is okay, but which way do I go? How do I get out of here?

The phone rings again, startling me out of my trance. I must get to it. Sheriff Blake and Gary are blocking the door while they trade punches, so that won't work.

"The window!" Zach shouts when he sees me searching for a way out. Irene aims her wand at me, forcing Zach to fire a counterspell, nearly knocking the wand from her hand.

"Thanks!" I shout, sprinting to the nearest window. Thankfully, it slides open easily, allowing me to slip out.

If Irene and Gary somehow prevail, I'm in big trouble. We're all in big trouble. Where is that blasted phone? I follow the ringing to a hollowed-out tree stump, shuddering when I realize I'll have to stick my hand in there. What if there's something icky inside? What if Irene has booby-trapped it with a spell?

Being held hostage by a demon and a witch is one thing. Touching creepy crawlies in the dark is entirely different. I hold my breath and close my eyes - as if that will help somehow - then thrust my hand into the stump. When I touch the cool steel of a phone and not a spider or a magical bomb, I breathe a sigh of relief, both for the phone and the lack of bugs.

I knew Irene wouldn't destroy it. I just knew it. Out of all the wacky stunts she's pulled so far, the one thing I knew I could count on was her wanting to keep proof of hers and Barney's relationship. No matter how ill-fated it was.

I pull the phone out, staring at it almost lovingly as I slide my finger over the cool, hard screen. After all this, I finally have it in my hands again. Proof that Anne didn't kill Barney.

Now I have to find Buster. If he's hurt, Irene better hope that it's Zach who bests her. If not, I will end her on the spot. Those two have caused my family enough grief this week to last a lifetime.

I sneak around to the front of the cabin, where the battle rages. I wish I could tell who's winning. I want to peek inside to see if there's anything I can do, but I have to find Buster first.

What if he's badly injured? What if he's out in the woods, wandering in pain all alone? What if he's lost? I can't bear to even think about it. I'm shocked and relieved when I discover him sitting patiently near the patrol car. Like he's waiting for a ride to the store. I can't believe the Sheriff let him ride in the car. That must have been a sight.

"Buster! Psst! Buster!" I whisper while he looks to and fro. When he finally sees me, he runs straight for me, loping excitedly in that comical, giant dog way of his. It's too late when I realize he isn't slowing down, though. He leaps on me, knocking me to the ground and licking my face.

"All right, all right, easy, boy," I tell him. "Let me up." When he finally backs up, I check him over carefully. The tender pink spot on his side could use some healing cream, which I can get from Anne's shop, but otherwise, it looks like he's okay.

"Did that mean ol' witch try to hurt you? Don't worry, where she's going, she won't be able to do this again." At least I hope so! The fighting noises in the cabin are louder than ever. I contemplate sneaking over to the sheriff's car to call for backup, but before I can make my move Sheriff Blake and Zach emerge triumphantly with Irene and Gary firmly subdued in magical handcuffs.

"You're both under arrest for the murder of Barney Mullins," Sheriff Blake says.

"You can't prove it!" Irene snarls, struggling to get away.

"Oh, yes I can!" I shout.

Irene sways like she'll pass out when I brandish the phone from my back pocket.

Gary whirls around to glare at her. "You could have thrown that thing in the lake. We could have run away to Mexico, spending the rest of our lives lounging on sandy beaches drinking mai tais. But ohhhh, no, you had to have those ridiculous messages from Barney. He never loved you anyway!"

When Irene lunges at me, Sheriff Blake grabs her to pull her back. I step backward, nearly dropping the phone.

"How about we hand this over right now?" Zach suggests, gently removing it from my hand to give it to Sheriff Blake.

"How soon can my sister get out of jail?" I ask him.

"I'll call Judge O'Malley on the way home and ask him to vacate her conviction."

"Ummm," Zach says like he's almost embarrassed to ask, but I understand. He wants his $10,000 back.

"Can we get Zach's bond money back?" I ask. "Arresting my sister was a big mistake after all. *Your* mistake." I add "respectfully, sir" when the Sheriff gives me the stink eye. It's true, though! It's not my fault he wouldn't listen to me.

But Sheriff Blake's crisp nod tells me that Zach will get his bond back, which is a relief. Not as big of a relief as getting my sister out of jail, but it's still a relief. Neither one of us wants to owe Zach $10,000, that's for sure.

We already owe him a huge debt of gratitude. $10,000 on top of that would be too much!

34

During the drive home, Buster leans forward from the back seat, sticking his enormous head between us. He hates to be left out. But when he says, "Can we stop at the coffee shop for some whipped cream?" I nearly wreck the car.

I'm almost afraid to look at Zach. If he heard nothing it will confirm I was hallucinating. Yet he stares ahead like he's afraid to move or even breathe. When he notices me staring at him, he finally blows out a breath of air. "You heard that too?" he asks.

"Yep," I squeak.

"Buster," I feel ridiculous asking this out loud, but we both heard it, so I can't be completely bonkers, "When did you start talking?"

He wrinkles his canine brow. "I've always talked."

"Uhhh, no, you didn't."

"I thought I saw one of Irene's spells hit him after the Sheriff ducked," Zach offers.

"It did. He yelped and ran off. When I checked to see if he was hurt, I found a pink mark on his side and told him I'd put some healing cream on it when we got home. Do you think Irene's spell made him talk?"

"I don't know how else to explain it." Zach shrugs. "Jake will freak when he finds out."

"I think *I'm* going to freak."

Before we can discuss this sudden development further, Harvey's name appears on the dashboard's call screen. I cringe. I almost don't want to know why he's calling. What if there was some crazy mix-up, and they won't let Anne out of jail after all?

"Aren't you going to answer that?" Zach asks.

"Harvey never has good news."

"But he must this time, right?"

"Don't count on it," I grumble, reluctantly pressing answer. This is almost as bad as sticking my hand into that dark tree trunk. "What's up, Harvey?"

"I have good news!" he shouts.

"Told you," Zach says, settling back in his seat with a smug grin.

If Harvey truly has good news, I don't even care that Zach was right.

"Zach and I are driving back from the cabin," I tell him.

"Hi, Harvey!" Zach says.

"Hey, guys," he responds.

"Hi, Harvey!" Buster shouts.

"Who is that?" he asks.

"It's a looooong story," I insist.

"Uhh, okay. You won't believe this, but Sheriff Blake called Judge O'Malley to demand an expedited release. Anne will be ready for you when you return to Melioras."

"Harvey, that's amazing! Thank you!" I exclaim.

"Don't thank me, thank the Sheriff."

"Do I have to?"

When we arrive at the prison gates, Anne is already there jumping up and down, waving at us. I didn't know they let prisoners out like that. I thought we'd have to cut through a ton of red tape before we took her home.

"If you stop by the courthouse tomorrow, Zach, they'll have a check for $10,000 waiting for you," she says the moment she gets in the car.

Buster is so excited to see her that he makes the SUV rock from side to side, his tail smacking against the leather seats and windows, is surprisingly loud. Anne good naturedly pats him on the side while dodging his drool. "Nice to see you too, Buster."

"I never doubted you," Zach responds.

"Of course you did."

"Okay, but just a little."

"Are we going to talk about why you confessed to two crimes you didn't commit?" I ask. I'm still steamed about that.

"Yeah, yeah, we'll get there eventually, but what I have to know right now is how Irene lured Barney to the house in the first place. Harvey only knew a little bit. He said you'd have the rest of the story for me. Did she just hide in the attic, waiting for him to appear so she could bash him on the head? This is all just so bizarre," she says.

"Irene and Gary are distantly related to Maureen Baker, Mr. Baker's niece. When Irene found out Maureen was selling the house, she asked her if she could show it to her fiancé."

"She really told her that?" Anne asks.

"She really did."

"She convinced Barney to come to the house where she was hiding, then jumped out and whacked him?"

"Nope. It's even more convoluted than that. She thought she could get Barney to come to the house with an offer to return his watch, then they'd start talking, and while she showed him the house, he'd realize how much he missed her and wouldn't it be great if they got married and bought it?"

"Yikes, that girl has problems. But assuming that didn't work?"

"She'd use a love spell."

"Obviously, none of those things worked."

"Nope."

"But how does Gary figure into all of this? I was so convinced he did it," Anne says.

"Just as Gary was leaving for the auction house in Tenebris Village, she told him what she planned to do."

"Oh, that's why he didn't make it up there."

"He went to the Baker house hoping to talk her out of it but caught Barney just as he was about to go inside."

"That's who the neighbor saw?" Anne asks.

"It sure was. He told Barney what Irene was up to and that he should just leave. He even promised he'd get the watch back for him if he'd go home and never speak to Irene again. Barney agreed, so Gary left because he still had to get to the auction house."

"Barney must have changed his mind."

"He did," I nod.

"How much longer will this story take?" Buster asks. "I want some whipped cream."

"Jumpin jehosaphat, did you hear that, or have I spent too much time in prison?"

"That's a spell gone wrong," I explain.

"Why do you keep saying that?" Buster asks. "I've always talked."

"No, you haven't," Zach and I respond simultaneously.

"As wild as this is," Anne points to Buster, "I need to know how the other soap opera turns out first."

"After Gary left, Barney changed his mind. He really wanted that watch back. He went into the house, and Irene convinced him to come to the attic. There's a beautiful view of the village from up there, and she thought it might inspire him to finally propose to her."

"Oh, boy."

"Molly, look, there's a coffee shop. Let's get some whipped cream!" Buster insists. Who knew the dog had a one-track mind?

"While Irene planned on a romantic reunion," I continue, "Barney was mad about the watch. When he found out she also kept one of the golf clubs, he blew up. There was a struggle, and she swung it at him, trying to get him to back off. She said she thought he would duck, but he never saw it coming. Then, blammo! The rest is history."

"So she took both his Rolex and one of the golf clubs almost like souvenirs?"

"Yes ma'am. Like a little pack rat collecting all things Barney."

"She must have called Gary again?" Anne suggests.

"She called Gary in a panic, telling him what she'd done. Gary called the auction house *again* to cancel for a family emergency, then raced back to the house. He wiped Irene's prints from the club, threw it in the bushes, and they ran."

"But not before taking Barney's watch."

"Indeed."

"So it was almost an accident that the golf club she used to kill him had my name on it."

"Unfortunately, yes."

"Does it sound weird to say I'd almost prefer that they set me up all along rather than it just being a lucky accident for them?"

"Not too weird. I mean, *you* did plead guilty to an accidental murder."

"You'll never let that go, will you?"

"Nope!"

"How do you know that all of this happened?"

"Gary told us everything," Zach says.

"But why?"

"After Sheriff Blake's backup arrived, and they started to haul them away, Gary realized he may go down for a murder he didn't commit. A murder he helped cover up, sure, but one he didn't commit. The story poured out of him," Zach says.

"Wow. This just gets crazier by the second. You know what else I keep thinking about? The first time we talked to Gary at the bar. He told us he was an hour away picking up the scotch for his boss when Barney was killed."

"Right," I respond.

"What if we told him that yes, we wanted to talk to his boss when he asked us? His alibi would have been blown then."

"Nope." I shake my head. "He said the only reason he offered that, was he knew his boss wasn't there anyway. He assumed we wouldn't ask and he was right."

"Oh man. That was a huge mistake on our part. But I'm still confused. This all happened, where?"

"At a cabin in the Steinley Forest that Mr. Baker owns."

"After refusing to believe us the entire time, how did you get Sheriff Blake on board?" Anne asks.

"Yes, Zach, I haven't thanked you yet for convincing the Sheriff to drive all the way up to the cabin. With you and Buster!"

"As much as I'd love to take credit for that, it wasn't me. It was Tina," Zach admits.

"Tina?"

"She is very persuasive."

“I know how she persuaded you,” I roll my eyes. “But how did she persuade Blake? She said pixie magic doesn’t work on werewolves.”

“They were high school sweethearts,” Zach says.

“What?” I nearly run the car off the road again. I have to be careful here. But that was almost as shocking as Buster talking. “She didn’t tell me that.”

“After she got a plumber to fix the broken pipe in her listing, she called me. She knew you’d ignore her advice and go alone. Next thing I know, we were driving to Steinley Forest.”

"I swear it will take me a month to process everything that's happened this week. I mean, what's next?" Anne asks.

"Whipped cream!" Buster shouts, smacking his tail against the window, trying to dance a happy jig in a vehicle not quite big enough to accommodate a giant dancing dog.

"All right, already we'll go to the coffee shop," I assure him.

I'm not sure I'll be able to process everything that's happened this week in my lifetime, forget doing it in a month.

35

"Jake! Get a move on! We're late!"

"Coming! Coming!" Jakes shouts, bounding down the stairs two at a time. Today he clutches both shoes to his chest while trying rather unsuccessfully to throw his backpack on with one hand. At least he combed his hair this morning. Kind of.

"Do you have everything you need?"

"Yep!"

"You know the hearing to reinstate my license is this morning, and then I have a showing this afternoon. If you forgot anything, it stays at home. No calling me to bring your homework, or your soccer gear, or your library book that was due yesterday."

"No worries, Mom, I got it covered," he says, resting a reassuring hand on my arm.

"Thank you."

"Hey, wouldn't it be weird if you found another body at the showing? That would make two in a row!"

"You want to walk to school, mister?"

Will Molly's real estate license be reinstated? Is there another body? Sign up for my email list at https://mailchi.mp/9ebce0da866a/email-signup-listto learn when The Lifeless Listing is released this year!

Or scan the QR code with your phone!

More Books by B I Skinner

Ghostly Glenwood Mysteries Paranormal Cozy Mysteries

The Case of the Haunted Hotel

The Case of the Pilfering Poltergeist

The Case of the Poached Peridot

The Case of the Gym Ghost(Pre-order)

Spooky Shanty Realty Mysteries

Afterlife in the Attic

The Lifeless Listing(Pre-order)

Marcall's Breakfast Cafe Paranormal Cozy Mysteries

An Eggscellent Day for Murder

24 Carrot Caper

Daggers and Donuts

Cupcakes and Corpses

A Crime of Cranberry

Peppermints & Pandemonium

Star Spangled Homicide

Blood Curdling Ballots

Sign up for my email list here

https://mailchi.mp/9ebce0da866a/email-signup-list

Follow me on Instagram **@bethiskinner** Facebook **@biskinner-author**

Cover art by Book Covers by Melody

www.ingramcontent.com/pod-product-compliance
Ingram Content Group UK Ltd.
Pitfield, Milton Keynes, MK11 3LW, UK
UKHW040007200726
13854UKWH00001B/78

9 798223 428848